GALAXYS
EDGE

IRON WOLVES

ORDER OF THE CENTURION

JONATHAN YANEZ WITH
ANSPACH + COLE

Edited by David Gatewood
Published by Galaxy's Edge Press

Cover Art: Fabian Saravia
Cover Design: Beaulistic Book Services
Interior Design: Kevin G. Summers

For more information:

Website: GalaxysEdge.info
Facebook: facebook.com/atgalaxysedge
Newsletter: InTheLegion.com

"The Order of the Centurion is the highest award that can be bestowed upon an individual serving in, or with, the Legion. When such an individual displays exceptional valor in action against an enemy force, and uncommon loyalty and devotion to the Legion and its legionnaires, refusing to abandon post, mission, or brothers, even unto death, the Legion dutifully recognizes such courage with this award."

98.4% of all citations are awarded posthumously.

To Michal Trojan Joseph Jr. (AKA Troy), 82nd Airborne Division, who gave his life for his country July 14, 1969, in Gia Dinh province, South Vietnam.

You'll never be forgotten.

—Your brother in arms, Al Yanez (AKA Bean)

CHAPTER 1

Six years before the Battle of Kublar.

"How bad is it?"

"Well, Sarge, it doesn't look pretty!" Doc, the legionnaire medic, yelled over the weapons fire impacting only a few yards beside them. "You want the bad news or the worse news?"

"Not the place or time, Doc." Sam gritted his teeth against the pain. "Get on with it!"

The blaster round had struck Sam in the vulnerable spot where the gray armor he wore on his right shoulder connected with his breastplate. The pain was somewhere between being branded with an iron and skewered straight through with a knife. But agony was something Sam had become used to. If the Legion had taught him anything, it was how to bottle pain and move on. What he was worried about was passing out and not being able to rejoin his brothers on the line.

"We're out of skinpacks," Doc said. "But I'm still going to have to stop the bleeding. I've got a flare I can use to cauterize the wound with, but it's going to make getting shot feel like a kiss on the cheek. This is going to kick you in the balls."

Sam propped himself up against the sandbags outside the palace. Not far to his left, the Iron Wolves held their ground despite a massive disadvantage in numbers. But they wouldn't be able to hold out for long.

"Just get me back into the fight, Doc."

"You got it." Doc reached for a thick red cylinder from a discarded ruck. "You want some pain meds before we do this? I know you want to stay alert…"

"No drugs." He considered asking for something to bite down on, but it wouldn't be wise to remove his helmet. He'd have to settle for roaring against the pain.

Private Rivera—"Bean" to his fellow leejes, a skinny kid new to the Wolves—shouted over the cacophony of blaster fire. "Doc, how's the sarge?"

"I'm good to go!" Sam lied. "I just need Doc to patch me up with one of his pink bandages, grab a lollipop, and then I'll rejoin the line."

"Roger that," Bean answered.

"I'm afraid I'm all out of lollipops, but I've got your pink bandage right here," Doc said, striking the flare. It burned to life, fighting off the gloom of the night. "Ready?"

Sam clenched Doc's free hand. "If I pass out, you get me up. That's not a request, that's an order."

Doc leaned over him. The flare burned so bright Sam would have had to look away had it not been for the tech in his helmet dulling the glow. "Howl to the moon if you have to, brother."

As the flame pressed against his flesh, Sam did just that, letting all the fiery agony he felt in his shoulder vent through his lungs. He had to fight off the fingers of unconsciousness that wrapped around his mind.

Finally the pain subsided. A cold curtain of sweat covered his face. "I gotta... I gotta take off this helmet. Just for a second."

Doc pushed Sam gently down. "Fine. Just stay behind cover." He examined the wound. "Not my best work, but it'll do. On the bright side, you'll have a nice scar to remember me by."

Sam grunted as he removed his helmet. Drops of rainwater ran down his face, mixing with his sweat. A dreadful odor assaulted his nostrils.

"Geez, Doc, what's that smell?"

Doc tapped his bucket. "My filters are working, so I don't smell it, but... I'm guessing that smell is you, brother. Nothing like the smell of your own burnt flesh, eh?" Doc grabbed his bag of depleted supplies. "All right then. Back to the line."

Sam put his helmet on and stood. "Thanks, Doc. Despite you lighting me like a cigar." He activated his vibro shield, and it hummed a deadly blue.

"Just doing my duty for the Legion we all know and love." Doc gave a quick salute and ran off.

Sam switched onto the main L-comm channel with a flip of his tongue. Captain Zeno's voice could barely be heard over the sounds of combat, but what he lacked in volume he made up for in sheer intensity. "Hold the line, you sons of war, hold the line! The rebels didn't know the

Iron Wolves carried death in their hands! Make 'em pay and KTF to the grave!"

"Oorah!" roared the few remaining Iron Wolves. The sound gave Sam goose bumps as he raced to join them.

"Let 'em hear it!" Captain Zeno shouted into his comms. "All helmets broadcast on full. Let 'em know death is coming for 'em!"

Sam rejoined the leejes as they roared into the night. It was clear every Iron Wolf still on his feet had turned his external speaker on full as they cried, "Oorah! Oorah! Oorah!"

CHAPTER 2

Seventy-Two Hours Earlier

Bean held his blaster rifle as though it were a microphone and looked into an imaginary camera. The rest of the Iron Wolves were gathered around, his devoted audience.

"Well, Troy," Bean began, doing his best impersonation of a deep-voiced holonews anchor. "I would usually open our interview with something along the lines of, 'Ladies and gentlemen, welcome to the show,' but since there are neither ladies nor gentlemen among us, I guess we'll settle for, 'Welcome, lost souls and those who've made poor life choices.'"

With a grin, Troy stepped up beside him and leaned over the barrel of the weapon, keeping up the illusion that it was a microphone. "That's right, Private Rivera. We're here with the legendary Iron Wolves this fine morning. Their poor life choices have led to them being shuttled to an Oba-forsaken planet on the fringe of Republic-controlled space. It's called Cononga, and I hear it's a lovely vacation destination."

There were laughs from the squad, and Sergeant Samson was happy to see it. After all they'd been through together, it was healthy for them to crack a few jokes. And he was pleased that they didn't mind joking around in front of their sergeant.

"You don't say." Bean looked to his fellow commentator. "And why are the almighty Iron Wolves being ordered to this lovely planet?"

"Well, Bean, I thought you'd never ask." Troy looked around the cramped shuttle space at the other legionnaires. "It seems we've been asked here by the ruling powers due to our reputation as loyal upstanding soldiers of the Repub—"

"Nope, nope," Bean said, interrupting. "I think you're reading from the wrong cue cards. That doesn't sound right."

"Oh, clumsy me." Troy shuffled some imaginary cards and began again. "It seems the ruling powers in the country of Cononga, which the planet takes its name from, have asked the Iron Wolves to be present for their official inclusion into the Republic because..." He peered at an imaginary card and raised an eyebrow. "Well, it seems that word of our exploits as legendary warriors has spread across the galaxy!"

"Oorah!" shouted the men in the shuttle.

Troy and Bean continued back and forth like this, going on about all the downtime and rest they could look forward to, and all the lovely women on the planet who were just dying to meet a real-life legionnaire. Of course, those things awaited only these few who were lucky enough to pull the job. Most of the Wolves had been left behind on board the *Breaker*. Only a squad-sized element was need-ed for the backwater ceremony.

And despite Bean and Troy's joking around, Sam knew this assignment really was an honor for the Iron Wolves. This was a big day for the country, if not the entire plan-et, which was years behind in terms of technology. This ceremony marked the moment when Cononga would be-come a formal ally of the Republic—the first step on the path to one day becoming a full member of the Galactic Republic—and they had chosen the Iron Wolves to help mark the occasion. Apparently the people of Cononga held warriors of the Wolves' caliber in high regard. Rumor was the leejes would be greeted almost as celebrities.

Still, Sam thought it was a strange assignment. His team was used to fighting in the toughest corners of gal-axy's edge, not doing what amounted to public relations work. But who was he to argue? A few days on a mission like this would be good for the men. They could use a little rest time before they were sent into yet another fight with some planet's inhabitants who were stepping out of line.

The holographic display screen sprang to life, and the men instantly quieted as Captain Zeno's image appeared on the screen, broadcasting from up front with the pi-lot. With his short-cut black hair, square jaw, and black eye patch across his right eye—he never told the story of how he'd gotten it—he had the look of a killer. Or maybe he simply *was* a killer, and no looks could hide that fact. There was a deadly presence to the man, and Sam was glad Zeno, rather than one of the Wolves' point lieutenants, was the officer in charge.

"Don't you all look like fine, upstanding Republic Legionnaires," Captain Zeno said.

Sam looked around at the men. They were kitted out with clean, new armor and weapons—a very uncharacteristic look for the Iron Wolves. It seemed the Senate only issued new equipment when men were going to be paraded around as a symbol of the Republic. When new equipment would actually save leej lives in a firefight... well, then budget concerns always seemed to come into play.

"Well," the captain continued, "*I* know better. But I still expect you all to be on your best behavior."

"Yes, sir," every throat in the room responded.

"Sergeant Samson." Captain Zeno looked to Sam. "I'll stay with the men once we land and make sure no one goes on any spur-of-the-moment joyrides. I need you to rendezvous with our guide and the representative the Senate has set up for us."

"Yes, sir," Sam replied, though internally he was less than pleased. *Great,* he thought, *I get to go rub shoulders with whatever clown the Senate has running this gig.*

Captain Zeno gave him a look that said he knew exactly what his sergeant was thinking. But it wasn't a stern look, it was an understanding one, with a twinkle in his one eye. "Good," he said. "Prepare for landing, men. We touch down in a few minutes." And he disappeared from the holographic screen.

Yeah, it was a good thing Zeno was the officer in charge. Sam had just regained his sergeant stripes after being busted down a rank—again. This time, he was determined to make it stick.

Troy looked over to Sam. "Sarge, you think we'll have to return our new armor and weapons when we get back? I mean, they had to fit us for it, so this gear is specific to all our bodies, right? I mean, anyone else who tries this on besides me is going to have a *ton* of room in the crotch."

Sam laughed. "Who knows what the almighty Republic has planned for us. Remember ours is not to ask why, ours is but to do and die."

"Oorah to that, sir," said Troy. He was looking at his brand-new N-4 with all the admiration of a historian holding a prized relic. "I just hope we get to keep the weapons at least."

"Troy! You gotta stop stroking your rifle like that..." Bean said. "It's getting weird, man." Though Bean was new to the unit, he and Troy already seemed like they'd been friends forever.

"You think everything's weird." Troy ran a hand through his Mohawk haircut. "You thought my haircut was weird, you think the way I get dressed in the morning is weird, and you think the way I eat is weird."

"You are kind of a weird guy," Doc chimed in. "I've seen you eat. The way you divide up all your food... it's unnatural."

"It's not right," Bean agreed.

Troy shook his head. "You guys are animals. Letting different kinds of food touch each other on the plate is barbaric. Might as well just mix it all up into a slop while you're at it."

"Your food thing *is* kind of weird, Private," Sam said with a grin. Usually he stayed out of these types of conversations, but he couldn't help himself this time around. "I think we should get you another full psych eval when we get back home."

Troy's jaw dropped. "*Another* psych eval? I never got my first one!"

A round of laughter warmed the shuttle, followed by a rumble of turbulence.

"Touch down in ten," Captain Zeno's voice thundered over the craft's speakers. "Buckle up."

Sam made sure his shoulder harness was secure, then quickly looked over all eight men in his squad. They were well-trained: harnesses were secured, helmets were stowed under their seats, weapons held in laps with the safeties on.

The shuttle shook again.

We're trapped in an impervisteel box floating through the sky on repulsors... Sam much preferred a firefight on solid ground to putting his fate in the hands of technology. But as always, he pushed the thought away.

The reverse propulsion engines whined, a harsh rocking motion announced their touchdown onto Cononga, and the shuttle doors opened.

Sam was always the first to exit. It was a rule he had with his men. He was the first to exit and the last to board. That was if he wasn't ordered otherwise. Captain Zeno was usually right beside him.

With his new helmet in one hand and his shiny N-4 in the other, he walked down the ramp onto the planet of Cononga and looked around.

To the left of the dirt airfield, he saw farmers bent over working rice paddies far into the distance. Beyond that was dense jungle. That fit the description he'd read of Cononga. It wasn't the tropical vacation paradise Bean and Troy kidded about, but an agrarian jungle planet whose primary export was rice.

To his right stood a hangar housing a seriously ancient, rust bucket of a starship. Once, it might have been a top-of-the-line fighter craft, but Sam would be surprised if the thing even started anymore. It looked like a relic of the Savage Wars—of the early Savage Wars, at that.

Next to the hangar was a single-story square structure that looked like an office. Sam started toward it as Captain Zeno and the rest of the Wolves unloaded behind him.

As he came near, shouting sounded from inside the office building. Sam's battle instincts kicked in, telling him to don his helmet and let its amplifiers tell him what was going on. Telling him to approach down the sights of his N-4.

Easy there, Sam coached himself. *It's just a diplomatic mission. No need to scare the locals.*

A deep guttural growl made Sam rethink that position. It sounded like a massive dog was inside the building. He thought for a moment to contact the captain—but to tell him what? That a stray puppy was on the loose?

He should have brought someone with him. He knew better than to scout ahead on his own. Even on a diplomatic mission, protocols existed for a reason. But he wasn't going back now and making some big deal about a dog.

He moved forward with his weapon at the low ready. The voice grew in volume, accompanied by the animal's baritone growls.

"I told you, Fenra doesn't go anywhere I don't go. We're a package deal." It was a stern voice. A woman. "I wouldn't push your luck with her either. She's not the forgiving type. And she says—well, I'm not going to tell you what she says because she needs to work on cleaning up her language. But it's not going to end well for you if you keep pushing the subject. We're together for a few days. Just deal with it."

A man's voice answered, officious but unsure. "I was not informed that our ambassador would be traveling with a full-grown lyconlore. I'll have to clear this with my superiors."

Sam reached the door, but didn't go in. He wasn't trying to eavesdrop, but he thought it wise to wait for the tension of the moment to die before knocking.

"You do whatever it is you gotta do, Glasses," the female said. "And by the way, Fenra says there's someone standing outside the door."

Sam took a step back. *Busted.* He cleared his throat and knocked.

"Hello? This is Sergeant Sam Samson with the Iron Wolves, Ninety-First Republic Legion. We just touched down and were told to meet our guide and contact here."

He'd never quite forgiven his parents for naming him Sam Samson. Either they had no imagination whatsoever, or they *really* liked the name Sam.

Feet and paws shuffled on the other side of the door, and a pungent odor made Sam's eyes water. He was tempted to put his bucket on.

The door unlocked and swung open. A hulking creature filled the doorway. From pointed ears to massive rear paws, it measured at least eight feet, and the dark gray fur covering its body did little to hide its substantial muscles. A long snout and yellow eyes greeted the sergeant.

Sam wasn't sure if he should say hello or aim his weapon at the beast.

"Well, come on in," the female voice said from somewhere behind the alien creature. "Or do you just want to stand there staring at each other?"

CHAPTER 3

"I, uh, no, I guess I'll come in." The sergeant squeezed through the door, pressing his body against the frame in order not to come too close to the massive creature staring at him like its next meal.

Beyond the doorway was what looked like a waiting room. A few uncomfortable looking chairs were set against the walls, and a table held scattered pamphlets. A woman lounged in one of the chairs, her dirty boots kicked up on the table, an ancient blaster rested low on her hip. She was leafing through one of the pamphlets, although it didn't look like she was actually reading it. In front of her stood a straight-backed man with prim glasses and a pristine haircut. His dark blue uniform and shiny black shoes clearly defined him as a Senate liaison.

"I'm Sergeant Samson with the Iron Wolves," Sam said. "I was looking for our local guide and the representative from the Senate?"

"Sergeant." The man stepped forward with a ready smile and an overaggressive handshake. "I'm representing the Senate here on Cononga. My name is Lyn Nix."

The liaison's palm was so smooth, Sam felt compelled to look down at the perfectly manicured nails. It had been ages since he'd seen skin free of any callouses. Lyn's hand made his own hand look like a paw.

Lyn nodded at the woman in the chair. "This is our local guide, Sola Kole, and her—errr…" He looked with unease at the massive creature still in the doorway. "Her *companion*. I was just discussing the possibility of leaving the creature behind when you—"

"I told you, we're a package deal."

Sola stood up and tossed the pamphlet on the table. Sam squinted at the title: *What Can the Republic Do for You?*

"Fenra comes with me, that's it," Sola said.

Lyn swallowed distastefully. "Well… I'm open to discussing this further. Perhaps Fenra can just stay a few steps behind us, or…"

The creature sidled up beside him, dwarfing him in size. It leaned down and looked directly into Lyn's eyes.

"Or she could just come," Lyn squeaked. "She can come with us, yes, that'd be just fine. Achoo!" He reached into a breast pocket and pulled out a handkerchief just in time to catch an onslaught of sneezes.

Of course this guy carries a handkerchief.

"Well," Sam said, "now that that's all squared up, the rest of my squad is ready and waiting outside."

"Great," said Sola. "Let's get this show on the road. The sooner we get this over with, the sooner we can all stop pretending to be friends."

"Not looking for friends, ma'am. Just hoping we can at least be civil." Sam extended his hand.

Sola stood a few inches shorter than him, but somehow seemed to be looking down at him. She ignored the proffered hand and patted him on the shoulder. "Friendship and trust are earned. But I agree, Legionnaire. We can play nice while you're visiting *my* sandbox."

She walked out the door.

Fenra seized the opportunity to grab Sam's still-outstretched hand, engulfing it with a huge, hairy paw. She gave it a single pump and then followed after Sola.

Lyn stepped up beside Sam. "I'm sorry about that." He spoke as if they were old friends sharing gossip. "I can request a different guide from President Gen. He and I are on very good terms."

"I don't think that's necessary," Sam said. "It's refreshing to have someone tell me exactly how they feel instead of lying to my face. If we can just get the... the—well, whatever Fenra is—to take a shower and maybe scrub her teeth, we'll be fine." He breathed through his mouth, wondering how long it would take for the smell of wet fur and bad breath to dissipate.

"Oh, right!" Lyn burst into a forced laugh and slapped him on the back. "Get her to wash. Good one, Sam!"

Sam raised his eyebrow and gave the man a stare. He didn't like being touched. Not by strangers, anyhow.

Lyn pulled back his hand. "Oh. Sorry about that." He cleared his throat and hurried out the door.

In Sam's experience, there were two types of representatives the Senate sent out to do their politicking. Those who straight up hated the Legion and didn't try to hide it, and those who seemed eager to try and make nice. To pretend there was a relationship that didn't exist.

Sam preferred the former.

Then again, maybe Sam shouldn't have been so hard-edged. It might have been fun to see the liaison play buddy-buddy with the rest of the Wolves. As Sam exited the building, he grinned at the thought of Lyn clapping Captain Zeno on the back.

He speed-walked to catch up with the others before they reached Captain Zeno and the rest of the squad, who appeared to be watching with some amusement the comical mix that approached.

Lyn trotted forward to arrive first. "Captain Zeno, I presume?" He extended a hand of welcome. "I'm Representative Lyn Nix. It's great to meet you and the rest of your party."

"Squad." Captain Zeno shook Lyn's hand.

"Excuse me?" Lyn pulled his hand away with a wince.

"We're a squad, not a party. I don't see any confetti or streamers here." He turned his one good eye to the hulking Fenra. "And what in Oba's good name do we have here?"

"This is Fenra," Sola said. "She's a lyconlore. I'm Sola. We'll be your guides while you're here on Cononga. There's a transportation truck on the other side of the office building. It's a short ride to the city."

As Sola, Captain Zeno, and Lyn settled into a logistics conversation, Sam felt the hairs on the back of his neck rise. Like he was being watched. Years of experience had told him to trust that feeling—and years of training had taught him to act naturally and not whirl around to search the perimeter. So he stood at ease and casually panned his gaze across the hundred and eighty degrees he could see.

Spotting nothing of interest, he scratched the back of his head, "accidentally" dropping his helmet in the process. He turned to pick it up, taking the opportunity to quickly scan the two buildings and the dense jungle beyond.

There was something there. A glint in the undergrowth.

Had his helmet been on, he could have called in what he was seeing through private L-comm to get some additional eyes. As it was, he couldn't look too obvious and risk spooking whoever was out there. He dusted off his helmet and gave one last glance into the foliage. Whatever had been there, catching the sun, was now gone. It was probably nothing. This wasn't a warzone, after all. It was some kind of House of Reason public relations stunt, having the legionnaires pose for pictures in their pretty, new armor. Sam was probably just seeing things and being overly paranoid, but a healthy dose of paranoia was what had always kept him sharp.

And alive.

Captain Zeno pounded a closed fist on the hull of the transport ship, giving them the all-clear to leave atmo and rejoin the Republic frigate waiting for them in-system.

"Sergeant Samson," he said. "A word before we hump it to the transport truck?"

"Yes, sir."

Sola and Fenra led the other leejes toward their ride. Sam noticed that although some of the leejes were checking their gear, quite a few were checking Sola's curvy figure instead. Lyn hurried alongside, trying to make awkward small talk with anyone in the squad who would make eye contact with him. He appeared to be having little success.

Sam fell in step beside the captain, and they brought up the rear, out of earshot of the others.

"You see them out there?" Captain Zeno asked quietly, looking straight ahead.

"I saw something," Sam answered. He forced himself to look away from the jungle and to the captain, like the two were having a normal conversation. "The sun caught glass, maybe a pair of macros or a scope."

"There were at least two, maybe more."

"Trouble?"

"Could be. Or it could just be locals wanting to get a glimpse of the Iron Wolves before the formal parade. We're supposed to be a big deal, remember? Called out here by Cononga's president himself. But my nose tells me that something doesn't smell right, and I'm not talking about the lyconlore."

"Should we tell the squad?"

Captain Zeno took a moment to consider the question. "They're all good leejes," he said. "They know not to let their guard down. Just remind them that they're still on the clock. Our mission isn't to patrol the jungles, and these sons of the Legion could use a few days' downtime. Let's hope they get it. But Sergeant... let's you and I keep our eyes open."

CHAPTER 4

The ride from the poor excuse of an airfield to the outskirts of Cononga's capital city was not at all what Sam had
expected for supposedly revered guests of honor. Instead
of rolling in a luxury sled with blackout windows, he and
the rest of his squad were piled in a large, open trailer
hitched behind a two-seater cab. Sola drove while Fenra
stuck her head out of the window and let the wind play
with her ears. To the squad's dismay, Lyn sat in the back
with the rest of them and chattered away about Cononga
and its history.

It wasn't even a repulsor-capable vehicle; dust clouds
kicked up behind them as they bounced hard along a
bumpy dirt road, which could barely be called a road.

The jungle pressed in thickly on both sides as if it had
plans to reclaim the ground it had lost. Sam tried to keep
an eye on their surroundings, but he couldn't see more
than a couple meters into the verdant foliage.

"… and that was the *second* time I was thrown in the
brig for indecent exposure and fighting on the same night,"
Troy said to Lyn, holding up a pair of fingers.

Sam smiled inwardly. The squad was apparently making a game of seeing who could get the Senate liaison to crack, grow indignantly offended, or flush with embarrassment.

"Well, you don't say?" Lyn chewed on his lower lip as if in thought. "I have a similar story. Once, when I was going through my schooling, I stayed up an entire hour past curfew. They said lights out at ten o'clock, but I didn't care! Well, I don't have to tell you, my instructors were less than pleased. I almost got written up for that one."

Bean ran a hand through his thick beard. "Dude... that's, uh, not the same at all."

"Wait, wait, that's not all of it!" Lyn raised his hands as if he was going to divulge a secret. "You didn't ask me *why* I stayed out an hour past curfew."

Troy and Bean looked to one another with amused smiles.

The silence lengthened.

"Why did you stay up?" Doc Dobson asked finally.

"I'm glad you asked, because this is going to be good." Lyn lowered his voice to just above a whisper. "I was meeting a girl. And not just any girl. *Jasmine Fox.*"

The men looked at one another confused. Clearly Lyn had thought this was a name everyone would immediately recognize.

Bean raised his hand. "She some kind of stripper, or...?"

"Oh, come now, gentlemen! Surely you've heard of *Doctor* Jasmine Fox?"

Blank stares looked back at him. No sign of recognition.

"So, like... was she hot?" asked Private Jarman.

Lyn looked to Captain Zeno for support. When the captain studiously ignored him, the liaison turned to Sam.

Sam only shrugged.

Lyn sighed with exasperation. "*Doctor* Fox is the leading mind behind the nanotech movement. She's the driving force that bolstered mechanized integration inside the Republic military!" He leaned back in his seat. "*That's* who Jasmine Fox is."

"You lost me at nanotechnology," said Troy.

"You lost me at who gives a sket," added Bean with a roll of his eyes. "Are you just making up fancy words to try and confuse us?"

"What? No." Lyn took off his glasses to clean them with his handkerchief.

Doc Dobson leaned forward in his seat. "I gotta say, I think Jarman got right to the heart of the matter. Was she hot?"

"She was that most rare of flowers." Lyn put his glasses back on.

All the men stifled a laugh at Lyn's choice of words. Sam even allowed himself a grin.

Only Captain Zeno remained stoic. He continued to survey the jungle, as diligent as ever.

Soon buildings began popping up on both sides of the road, in vivid blues and bright oranges. It seemed the Conongan government didn't have much in the way of zoning laws, as homes and shops stood intermingled without any semblance of districts or planning. Wherever the jungle could be beaten back to make room, some sort of structure had taken its place.

The local populace waved and shouted to them with bright smiles and eager eyes as they passed. It seemed the entire city, from the youngest child to the oldest grandparent, had come out to welcome the legionnaires. Some ran alongside the vehicle, grinning like maniacs. They really were being treated as celebrities.

Sam found the whole thing disconcerting. Put him in a trench taking enemy fire, and he knew exactly what to do. But to actually be *welcomed* by the locals...it just didn't feel natural. So he scanned the crowd, doing his best to try to pick out any signs of trouble: people watching from back in the shadows, scowling faces, bulges under a shirt or beneath a waistband.

"So," Lyn shouted over the noise of the vehicle and the crowd, "as you can see, we've entered the outskirts of the capital city of Noi. We're headed for the palace steps, where the president will be waiting. We'll have a brief run-through so we all know how it's going to go at tomorrow's official signing. You're going to have a grand time! As you can see, the people of Noi are *thrilled* to have you here. The reputation of the Iron Wolves precedes you!"

Bean stood up, laced his fingers, and shook them on either side of his shoulders like he had won an award. The others laughed and seemed to be enjoying all the attention from the locals. Most waved and smiled at the adoring crowd. The scene was straight out of a House of Reason public relations holo.

But Sam still felt uneasy. Somehow, he just couldn't enjoy playing the part of a hero. *Maybe because you know the real heroes are gone. The real heroes are the reason you're even here today.*

Sola managed to avoid hitting any of the pedestrians as she moved through the narrow streets—an impressive feat, given that the dense crowd seemed never to have learned the basic rules of road safety. Eventually the brakes screeched, and they came to a halt in a statued courtyard with a grassy knoll at its center. A long, stone stairway led south to iron gates that protected an important-looking building with white domed roofs. That had to be the presidential palace.

Captain Zeno jumped off the back of the vehicle, barking orders. "Keep it tight, eyes open. We're here to work, not on a vacation."

The leejes followed suit, and Sola and Fenra fell in step alongside them. Lyn led them through a crowd of well-wishers, who respectfully parted to make way. As they approached the iron gates, Cononga soldiers, dressed in green military fatigues and carrying outdated rifles, opened the gates and saluted them.

Sam gritted his teeth. There were too many people, and the chatter, in a broken dialect that almost, but not quite, resembled Sam's own, was grating to his ear. Worst of all, with his N-4 in his right hand and his helmet in his left, if things went bad he'd be a few seconds late in reacting. And a few seconds could mean the difference between giving, or taking, a blaster round to the skull.

Put your bucket on.

He wanted to. But if he did, the men would feel obligated to do the same. And they were supposed to present a friendly face to the locals—not faceless visors.

"Sir! Iron Wolf!" A boy was fighting his way through the ocean of people, trying to capture Sam's attention. "Sir!"

Sam drifted to the edge of the procession and looked down at the little one. The kid was skinny without being sickly. His fair skin and white hair were coated with a fresh layer of dirt, probably from running alongside the vehicle. He couldn't be more than twelve.

The boy pointed to Sam's left shoulder—to the emblem of their squad marked on his armor. A snarling wolf.

"You are a Wolf!" the boy declared, with wide eyes full of wonder. "You're an Iron Wolf!"

"That's right," Sam said. He scanned the area in case this was some kind of ploy. He had faced enemies who were not above using children as decoys, or even as human shields. "I'm an Iron Wolf."

The boy's mouth dropped open. He reached out as if to caress the emblem, then, remembering himself, pulled his hand back. "I'll be an Iron Wolf one day, too."

"I don't doubt it," Sam said with a smile.

He continued with the squad up the stone steps that led up to the palace entrance. Lyn stopped them at a broad plaza about halfway up, where more Conongan soldiers were doing their best to keep the populace back and in order.

Above, guards on either side of the entrance opened the black metal doors for an overweight man with a ready smile. He descended the steps to them with open arms.

"Welcome to the capital city of Noi! I am President Van Gen, and we are so honored you have come to be present as we enter partnership with the Republic. I have no doubt that as the nation of Cononga goes, so will the rest of Cononga. Soon the entire world will join the illustrious Galactic Republic!"

The part of the crowd that was within earshot cheered at this announcement, and soon the enthusiasm swept to the rest in joyful revelry, whether they knew what had been said or not.

Sola and Fenra stood off to the side while Lyn gave a slight bow before sweeping his arm out to introduce the legionnaires. "President Gen, this is Captain Zeno and the Iron Wolves. Captain Zeno, this is President Gen."

Captain Zeno extended a hand with a tight nod. "President Gen, thank you for having us."

Sam looked out across the gathered throngs. From this elevated vantage point, Sam could see to the tops of the surrounding buildings. A glint of sunlight caught his eye from the roof of a building to his left, no more than a half kilometer away. He studied the spot. There was a figure there, dressed in black, holding a pair of binoculars. As Sam watched, the figure motioned to someone in the crowd below.

Sam felt his stomach twist into a knot. He could already see what was about to happen, and he was too late.

Two men in the crowd threw back long robes, revealing shiny new blasters. They aimed them at the president.

CHAPTER 5

Time slowed as Sam's training kicked in.

"Hostiles, eight o'clock!"

He went to a knee. His helmet fell on the step next to him as his weapon rose to his eye.

"Get down!"

He took in every detail of his targets as he lifted his N-4, but could make out little; the two men in the crowd were draped in baggy clothing that shrouded their features.

The shooters' shiny blasters couldn't have fired many rounds in their short existence, but they fired now. The familiar whine split the air as yellow shots erupted through the gathered crowd.

Sam released the breath from his lungs. He refused to let the adrenaline coursing through his veins cause him to make a mistake.

One shot. He repeated the old mantra in his head. *One kill.*

Screaming filled the square. Panicked revelers fled in terror.

Sam lined up his first target and immediately took the shot. He adjusted his blaster rifle with a quick exhalation, and took down the second shooter a half second later. Both targets fell in what was now a churning mass of bodies trying to escape. In situations like this, more people would be killed from trampling than from blasters.

Sam looked behind him to see what damage the shooters had done before he had eliminated the threat.

A few scorch marks lined the steps of the palace, but no one was harmed. But there was no time to feel relief.

"More hostiles!" cried Private Moon.

Sure enough, multiple shooters, all dressed in the same loose clothing, were now popping up all over the square.

A pair of Iron Wolves—Thompson and Jarman—assisted the local security in rushing President Gen inside. The other legionnaires slammed on their helmets and brought their weapons to bear.

With the president out of range, the hostiles now focused their blaster fire on the legionnaires. Bolts flew from a dozen different directions.

Sam grabbed his helmet and slammed it on his head. Captain Zeno was already barking orders over the L-comm.

"Fall back behind our ride!" Captain Zeno snapped. "I want suppressing fire. And choose your targets carefully. We aren't here to kill kids."

As Sam moved toward the vehicle, a round hit him in the left shin. It felt as though he'd been struck with a seamball bat. Even with the armor's protection, Sam's leg buckled, and he lost his balance on the palace steps, but he smoothly turned his fall into a roll and tumbled down.

When he leapt to his feet at the bottom of the stairs, his weapon came up with him.

He sighted another hostile running toward them. This one was wearing a vest dangling with grenades. He probably wasn't the same dude that shot Sam in the shin... but he would have to do.

Sam took a second to aim, then squeezed off a round. It hit the soldier dead center on his chest, and his explosive vest detonated.

A shock wave of grisly carnage rolled across the square. As Sam lowered his head to weather the storm, he checked on his injured shin. It hurt like hell, but the shiny new armor the Senate had provided to showboat them around in was the real deal, top-of-the-line stuff. It had absorbed the shot in a way that his previous kit, worn down from too long use, never could, even if it was the same model.

I guess those no-good silver spoons at the Senate are good for something.

Small-arms fire sizzled through the air as the Iron Wolves called out targets, assembling a cohesive, and lethal, counterfire. Each leej moved from target to target in a seemingly never-ending series of kills.

"Hit you in the leg?" Doc asked, coming to a skidding halt beside Sam.

"I'm whole." Sam didn't even look over at the corpsman; he was too busy sending a volley of fire at the top of an enemy's head peeking over the edge of a roof. "This shiny dress armor can take a hit."

"Roger that. Can you make it to the cover of the truck?"

"Let's go." Sam rose to his feet.

He had to force his legs to move. His right shin felt like it was going to give out on him with every step. It throbbed with a deep ache. The bone was bruised.

Being a legionnaire had taught Sam all kinds of fun stuff—like how to kill an enemy with his bare hands. It had also taught him how to deal with pain. How to recognize it, but not dwell on it; how to look past it to the next task that needed doing.

Right now, Sam focused on reaching the cover of the truck a few dozen yards away.

Scores of unlucky locals writhed in pain across the square, but the area was mostly cleared of fleeing civilians, leaving the Iron Wolves, a few members of the local militia, and the insurgents, to shoot it out without risk of further collateral damage.

Sam rounded the vehicle and slammed into the cab area with the rest of his squad. All ten of the legionnaire diplomatic contingent were present.

"You good, Sergeant?" Captain Zeno asked via the comms. "Time to take it to these cowards!"

"Oorah that, sir," Sam said, quickly looking over his men. If any of them were injured, they didn't show it. They were finding firing lanes through the open back of the vehicle or around it, keeping the insurgents from getting any closer. "Orders?"

"You all should coordinate with the Conongan militia," Sola shouted, her blaster in her right hand, taking shots at the attackers, as she backpedaled around the front of the vehicle to take cover with them. Her beastly partner was nowhere to be seen. "Better to get them on the same plan as you instead of running into each other's firing lanes."

"Who's attacking us?" Captain Zeno's voice was the polar opposite of Sola's. Where she was sarcastic—almost complacent—the captain was intense and ready to kill. "What do they want?"

"Beats me," Sola answered.

"Not good enough." Captain Zeno's voice was as cold as a steel knife. "Try again."

"If I had to guess, they're part of a separatist faction in the north. Just radicals. Didn't think they had the credits to buy weapons, much less start a war." Sola managed to sound indifferent even as she shouted to be heard over the sound of blaster fire.

"Get the Conongan militia to take the left side of the square," Captain Zeno said to her. He looked over at Sam. "Sergeant, go with her and coordinate from their position."

"Roger that, sir." Sam popped off a few more rounds over the hood of the vehicle. "Ammo's already running low, sir. We didn't expect to get into a fight."

"Conserve the charge packs you have."

"Yes, sir." Sam gave Sola a nod. "I'll follow you. This is your backyard. You know where we're going?"

Sola scanned the square with her bright blue eyes. She pointed to a building on their left where a group of Conongan militia had taken cover. "That's Colonel Minh. Let's go there."

"Okay, keep low," Sam said. "Where's Fenra?"

As if in answer, a bloodcurdling scream rose above the sounds of weapons fire. Sam had heard a man scream like that only once before, on a backwater planet out on the edge, when some nightmarish jungle creature found a local and ripped him in two.

"Fenra prefers to do her killing up close," Sola said with a grin. "Follow me."

They took off in a low, crouching run.

"Let's give them some cover," Captain Zeno barked. "But only shoot at what you can hit."

While Sam ran with Sola to the Conongan militia, Captain Zeno's voice continued speaking on a private channel that included only Sam and the starship orbiting the planet.

"*Breaker,* this is Captain Zeno, come in."

"Captain Zeno, this is Major Roy, go ahead."

Sam groaned inwardly at the name. Major Roy was a point puppet, a privileged elite from the House of Reason who had never seen actual combat or even sent any kind of strike against the enemy.

"Major Roy." Captain Zeno remained calm despite the chaos around him. "We've encountered a group of hostiles. Requesting immediate reinforcements and a tactical strike on three Cononga buildings being used as firing positions. Grid coordinates Hex—"

"Captain Zeno," the major interrupted, "you are on a peaceful mission. You are not authorized to engage the populace. I repeat, *do not* engage the populace." He spoke less like an officer than a teacher telling a child why he was supposed to walk, not run, around the pool. "Cease fire immediately."

"To hell with that!" Captain Zeno's calm was gone. "We are *taking* fire and require air support and reinforcements as soon as possible. This little diplomatic ceremony has gone to the nine hells."

Silence.

"Major!" Captain Zeno shouted. "My men are going to *die* if you don't make this happen!"

"Stand by." Major Roy spoke as if he were being woken from a dream. "I'll have to get clearance from my superiors. In the meantime, I'm... I'm ordering you to remove yourself from the altercation."

"You're what?"

"These internal affairs on Cononga can be... sticky."

"Yeah, roger that."

Sam and Sola finished their run, diving for cover around the building. They joined the rest of the pinned-down Conongan militia, who were keeping low to avoid a torrid volley of blaster fire.

Captain Zeno ended the transmission, then spoke to Sam on a private comm. "All right, Sergeant. Point or no point, I'm not letting anyone shoot at the Wolves and get away with it. If Major Roy needs some time to figure things out, we'll give it to him, but *we* know what needs to be done right here, right now."

"I'm with you, sir," Sam replied in between panting breaths. "Let's take it to 'em."

CHAPTER 6

Sam took a quick appraisal of the man Sola had pointed out as the leader of the Conongan militia. Colonel Minh was surprisingly young, perhaps early thirties, and his eyes were every bit as wide as those of the young, awe-struck boy Sam had talked to on his way up the steps of the palace. With one distinct difference: Colonel Minh's eyes were saucers of fear.

Sam had seen that look a dozen times before, some-times in the eyes of his own men, more often in the eyes of their enemy. The dazed look of confusion.

He quickly scanned the handful of soldiers with him. Most were holding it together better than their leader, but their ill-fitting green fatigues and helmets—Minh's was so small it covered only the dome of his head—told Sam ev-erything he needed to know about the Conongans's level of military preparedness.

For a culture so enamored with warriors like the Iron Wolves, it struck Sam as odd that they would appear to be so inept when a fight broke out. Clearly there was some-thing more to these Conongans.

"Hey!" Sam shouted at the colonel. "You in charge here?"

Colonel Minh mumbled something inaudible, without making eye contact.

The man was not exactly inspiring his men. As they looked at their frozen leader, Sam could see whatever courage they had melting by the second.

The day you are destined to die is already set for you. Sam took a deep breath as he reminded himself of this truth. *You're a legionnaire. You're already dead.*

He rose to his feet, ignoring the enemy weapons fire that slammed into the corner of the building not a yard from his position. Unless the insurgents had a tank, the wall would keep them protected—for now. He grabbed Colonel Minh by the collar, yanked him to his feet, pressed him hard against the building... and slapped him hard across the jaw.

The Conongan militiamen cried out in surprise. They looked to one another as if seeking direction, and Sam saw a few fingers tighten around weapons, as if these men might just do something about their colonel being smacked around.

Sola casually waved her blaster at the group. "Easy there, cherries. Give him a chance. He's a legionnaire, remember?"

Sam reminded himself to thank Sola after this was all done. She, at least, seemed to understand that their lives might depend on instilling a shred of courage into this shaking colonel.

"Listen to me, Colonel," Sam said harshly. "I don't have time to get to know you. I can't find out why you fight, who you fight for, or what will push you in the right direction to be the leader you're called to be right now. What I *can* do is tell you that your brothers need you. *Now.*"

He stepped back and gestured to the other Conongan soldiers.

Minh turned his face toward his men, and the fog over his eyes cleared a bit. A thin line of blood trickled down the corner of his split lip. Sam had really walloped him.

"Now, me and the Iron Wolves, we're here to help you. You're not alone. We have your back." Sam released the colonel. "But you *need* to get it together. If not for yourself, then for your men. We gotta get in this fight. Are you with me?"

Colonel Minh nodded.

"Say it!" Sam clapped the colonel hard on the shoulder. "Tilt your head back and yell it to the sky. Let the enemy know we're coming for 'em!"

"I'm with you," Colonel Minh said, with a hard Conongan accent.

"Louder!" Sam roared.

The colonel didn't tilt his head back, but bellowed right in Sam's face. "I'm with you!" he screamed.

"Yeah, you are," Sam said, nodding in approval. The colonel's eyes were clear now. Fear was still very much present, but as long as his desire to take action was stronger than that fear, he would be all right.

"We're moving on the right," Captain Zeno said over the comms. "This is going to get ugly. We'll have to take them out building by building. Status?"

"We're about ready to move," Sam replied. "I'm organizing the Conongans now."

"Roger that. Let's hurry it up and go to work."

Sam switched back to his bucket's external speakers as he addressed the colonel. "How many of your men are ready to fight right now? We need to clear the left side of the square. We'll go building to building."

"I... I don't know. I think ten, maybe twenty men scattered around the outside of the next two buildings." Minh reached for an antique comm at his belt. "I can call the rest of them to our location now."

"You haven't already done that?" Sam tried to keep the shock out of his voice, but it was impossible.

"No. We've never been in an engagement before. The Cononga militia is only a few hundred strong, and that includes local law enforcement and palace guards."

"I'm sorry, I think I misheard you. I thought you just said 'a few hundred.'"

"That is what he said," Sola replied. She peeked around the corner and quickly ducked back as a hail of weapons fire peppered the spot where she'd been. "Welcome to Cononga, Sergeant Samson. Just because they esteem the Iron Wolves doesn't mean they're ready to join the Legion."

The woman seemed to actually be enjoying this. A small smile tugged at the corner of her lips.

"You're damaged goods, lady." Sam shook his head, then stared Colonel Minh straight in the eyes. "Okay, Colonel. Let's work with what you have. I'll take the lead clearing the building, with you and your men covering my six."

"Okay, we can do that," the colonel said. "But what is your six?"

Holy universe on fire, I'm going to die today.

"My rear, my back," Sam said. "Make sure no one shoots me in the back."

"Oh, okay, Wolf. You got it." Colonel Minh motioned to his soldiers. "We follow the Wolf into battle. Legionnaires don't die."

"I wish that were the truth," Sam said, too low for anyone to hear except Sola, who stood right next to him.

"I got you," she said with a wink. She pulled a handkerchief up to cover the lower half of her face. "It's a good day to die."

"You people have twisted views of death," Sam muttered, wondering exactly who this woman was. He then shouted so all the militiamen could hear. "Okay, cover fire on my go. Three, two—Wait, you know what cover fire is, right?"

"Yes, yes of course." Minh nodded excitedly. On the plus side, the man's fear seemed to have completely vanished. He looked ready to fight. "You run in, and we pew-pew the enemy with our weapons."

"Pew-pew, huh?" Sam couldn't help but grin.

"Yes, pew-pew." Colonel Minh appeared not to realize this was funny to Sam. "Kill the rebels. Pew-pew."

"All right," Sam said, "pew-pew on my go." He started the countdown again. "Three, two—"

Before he could finish, Sola jumped out from behind the building corner firing her blaster.

Great. It's going to be one of those days, Sam thought.

He turned the corner with the sight of his N-4 already aligned with his helmet's visor. The weapon was an extension of his movement. Wherever his line of sight traveled, so did the N-4's barrel.

Yellow blaster fire skipped and sizzled around him, but there were only two things in his mind: *find the target, kill the target.* He ducked low, sighting a pair of black-clad men on a rooftop two buildings down. They were sending down plunging fire with heavy blasters. Exhaling, Sam pulsed a controlled burst to put down the first target. Three red blaster rounds struck center mass, and the man fell from the roof face-first into the unforgiving, hardened dirt street below.

From the periphery of his vision, Sam saw Sola kick in a door to the building on their left. Her blaster blazing, she went inside. The woman had courage—or foolhardiness—but she was going to get killed if she didn't coordinate and wait for backup.

Sam wanted to move and help her clear the building, but there was still another shooter on the rooftop, and the man had ducked low upon seeing his buddy drop. Suddenly, his shoulders and head appeared as he pulled his arm back to lob a grenade, but Sam had a clear shot.

The rebel took blaster bolts to the sternum, throat, and face. He slumped out of sight, but the grenade still managed to tumble down over the wall.

Sam rolled to the left, toward the building Sola had just stormed, but he was still very much in the open.

"Ah, hell!" He hurled himself through the doorway, heedless of what might be waiting on the other side.

BAM!

The grenade's explosion helped send Sam sailing over the threshold. It must have been some kind of a shock weapon, because no shards or projectiles accompanied the blast. He was still in one piece.

That was good.

One piece was good.

He got to his feet and looked around. He was in a store. Shelves around him were full of foodstuffs and accessories, though someone—probably Sola—had left more than a few scorch marks on the inventory.

"Sola," Sam called out, not wanting to surprise her and get himself shot for the trouble.

He received no reply.

The audio enhancers in his helmet picked up the sound of someone struggling. The sound was coming from a doorway in the back of the store.

Sam moved forward cautiously, weapon up, his head on a swivel. He passed from the store into another room—an office. The sounds of struggling had stopped.

Had those been the sounds of Sola? She should never have gone in alone. Clearing a building solo was what stupid people did. She should have had some of the militia with her.

So, for that matter, should he.

As he came around a cabinet, revealing more of the office, he saw Sola standing by the far wall, her blaster pistol pressed against the forehead of an enemy soldier. The man was in dark robes, but beneath them was a black uniform. So—these guys were organized. Paramilitary at a minimum.

"Oh, good," Sam began, and stepped forward.

Only then was he in position to see the other black-clad enemy. This one stood right behind Sola with his own rifle aimed at the back of her head.

Sam's reaction was immediate. He aimed his N-4 at the second man, and fired.

Nothing happened.

Sam took a heavy breath and felt his pucker factor go off the charts. *Of course you'd run out of ammo right now.*

The rebel soldier showed surprise—whether from Sam having an empty charge pack or just because he wasn't expecting company, Sam couldn't say—but quickly spun so his blaster rifle was now fixed directly on Sam.

"No chance you believe in a fair fight, is there?" Sam said.

The soldier gave a war cry and squeezed his trigger.

CHAPTER 7

There was no time to think. There was barely time to react.

As the rebel opened fire, Sam threw his N-4 at the man, trusting in his armor and providence to keep him alive.

The armor, it turned out, could take the day off. The rebel's shots went wide left as he ducked instinctively when the rifle came twirling toward his head.

Sam lowered his shoulder and slammed into the man with every ounce of force he could muster. The impact of the armored battering ram sent both men to the floor, with Sam landing on top.

The rebel had, however, maintained hold of his weapon. Sam grabbed the man's wrist, denying him the opportunity to fire, and the two men struggled, the rebel pushing and slapping at Sam's helmet while Sam looked for anything he could use as a weapon.

A brick-sized rock lay next to a side door—presumably there to be used as a doorstop. Sam grabbed it with his free hand and struck the rebel's face as hard as he could.

The man's skull split wide in a spray of dark red blood. It was an instant kill.

But Sam didn't stop. Over and over and over again, he lifted the rock and brought it down on the man's face, turning his head into a barely recognizable mush of flesh and blood with slick tufts of gory hair sprouting forth here and there.

You're losing it again, Sam! Said a quiet voice somewhere from the back of his mind. So distant and small that it could barely be heard. *Sam... you're getting lost! Sam! Sam!*

The voice was drowned out by the rage.

Crimson red droplets coated Sam's armor by the time he heard Sola screaming for him to stop. He finally snapped out of the trance—a trance like so many others that had impacted his career in the Legion.

"Sergeant!" Sola yelled. "I don't want to interrupt the issues you're working out right now, but we have company!"

Sam's lungs burned. He could hear the tiny fans pumping cool air inside his bucket; his helmet was already delivering additional oxygen to compensate for his exertions. He looked to the rock in his hand, dripping with blood, still held high for yet another strike. He let it slip from his hands. It tumbled away from the bloody pulp below him, leaving oblong stamps of blood as it rolled.

Sam forced himself to stare at what he'd wrought— just for a moment.

Then he regained awareness of his surroundings.

Sola had dispatched the other rebel soldier in a much less grisly, though no less lethal fashion. But now more trouble was coming. Shadows danced beneath the side door—multiple pairs of feet obscuring the bright sunlight that shone through the crack.

Sam was still half in the rage-fueled zone he'd allowed himself to enter. The one he told himself he *needed* in order to survive, in spite of his instructors, and a good number of fellow leejes, telling him otherwise. Telling him to remain frosty and KTF. His heart was racing. Adrenaline pushed through his body like heavy ink through a glass of water.

A shot sounded from the other side of the door, then a body slammed into it. They were attempting to break it down.

Sam didn't see where his N-4 had landed, so he grabbed the dead rebel's weapon. A bright black pistol with a wide barrel. Probably ate up charge packs like candy.

BAM!

The door was kicked in.

Sola fired from behind the cover of a desk, dropping two men with shots to the chest and head before they could even enter the room.

Sam hadn't had time to find cover, but as more rebels spilled through the doorway, he hunched down, making himself as small a target as possible, and pumped blaster bolt after bolt at the oncoming enemy.

Although he had snapped out of the trance, it wasn't far. The rage was so close he could feel it breathing down his neck, and he immersed himself in the moment. He didn't worry how much ammunition the rebel weapon held, or if it would overheat. All he could think about was putting these rebels down, one after the other. He's was slipping, losing control again...

And it was working. The rebels stopped trying to storm the room and opted instead to fire into it from positions of cover outside.

He hoped they didn't have any fraggers on them.

Sola cried out in pain from her spot behind the desk, and went down.

The rebels apparently took this as a sign to attempt another charge. Sam took out the first man the moment his head appeared in the doorway, but right after the trigger pull, the weapon beeped to indicate an empty charge pack.

"Oh, for crying out loud."

Sam reached down for his own sidearm, and found the holster empty. So he pulled his knife from his webbing. The blade was six inches long, with one serrated edge capable of cutting through leej armor. He was prepared to go down fighting.

The rebels were holding back once more, but it would only be a matter of time before they made another charge.

Sam looked over at the Conongan guide. "Sola. You all right?"

Sola propped herself up. Pressed her right hand to her left thigh, gave Sam a gritty grin, then reached for her fallen blaster and nodded to the door. "Heads up," she said. "Incoming."

A cautious rebel peered into the room, tentatively stepping over his dead comrades that littered the doorway. No headlong charge this time. Apparently between Sola's cry in pain and the absence of blaster fire coming from inside, the rebels were optimistic the way might be clear.

Sam sprang from his crouched position, grabbed the rebel's blaster muzzle, and turned it away as he bullied the rebel back. The rebel struggled to regain control of his rifle, and Sam took the opportunity to stab him repeatedly in the gut.

The strength of Sam's assault sent the two men through the open doorway, the rebel stumbling, horror-stricken, and Sam senselessly out for blood. He realized at once he had made another in an epic series of mistakes as soon as they emerged into an alley.

Four rebel soldiers stood waiting with blasters, but Sam's only weapon was a knife. He'd be dead already if these men weren't so stunned by his sudden appearance and the gory demise of their comrade by his hand.

He was committed now. His rage had taken him too far. His only hope was to take the four rebels in a surprise charge. To fight so close to them that the knife would be the superior weapon. Close enough that the rebels, who hardly seemed like seasoned soldiers, would fixate on not being cut instead of finding a way to put him down.

Pouring everything he had into his pumping legs, Sam lunged forward, screaming like a beast, his bloody knife leading the way. In an instant, he was in their midst, employing the skills developed through years of hand-to-hand combat training. He reacted to each movement of his enemy, closing ground when they tried to back away, slashing arms when they attempted to grab hold. To stay still was to die. So he kept moving, lunging, slicing, feinting, and his heart pounding from the constant exertion.

The first man went down with an upward cut into the stomach. Sam ripped the knife tip up and out, then spun and plunged it into the neck of a rebel coming at him from the right.

Halfway there.

Hands reached out for him. Sam felt the butt end of a rifle crack against his armored head.

On pure reflex, Sam whirled around, threw a left cross at the rebel who'd clubbed him, and with his right hand drove his blade deep into the ribs of the fourth soldier.

Had there been only four soldiers, Sam would have been victorious, but reinforcements appeared from the alleyway's end.

Before Sam could lash out again or grab a fallen soldier's weapon, rough hands grabbed his right arm, keeping his knife at bay, and rifle butts pounded his skull. It was better than taking a blaster bolt to the gut—apparently they wanted to take him alive—but it sent him reeling, and he finally went down hard onto his back when an enterprising rebel kicked him in the back of his knee.

More blows rained down on him. They were finding gaps in his armor now, and the pain fueled his rage. He struggled to get up, shouting, "I swear I'll kill you all!"

Someone stepped on his hand, forcing him to lose his grip on the knife.

"Get him up," a voice ordered. The accent was not like the halting speech of the Conongans. It was smooth, with a Mid-Core polish. "Take off his helmet."

Sam was lifted off his feet and slammed roughly against the building's wall. His helmet was yanked from his head.

He blinked against the unfiltered daylight. His body ached in a dozen different places, but beyond the pain was the desire to see who was giving orders to these Conongan rebels.

His gaze came to rest on an aline. Sam had never liked the looks of this species. Their light green skin might have made them attractive if not for the flappy fingers of skin hanging off their upper lips, like some kind of fleshy mustache.

The aline smiled. "It's been a long time since I've crossed paths with a legionnaire. What did you think you were going to do? Stab us all, one by one?"

"The thought crossed my mind," Sam said, with a smile of his own. "Or I could chuck the knife and just use my hands. Might actually prefer it that way. Why don't you tell your—"

The stranger was so fast, Sam didn't see the strikes coming. A fist that felt like a brick landed across the left side of his jaw, and another made contact over his right eye.

"The legionnaires I knew were tactical and deadly," the aline snarled, his voice dripping with contempt. "You fight like an undisciplined, angry child."

Pain exploded in his head, and the familiar metallic taste of blood filled Sam's mouth.

At that moment, an almost unbearably foul odor found its way to his nose.

"He has loosed his bowels!" yelled a disgusted rebel.

Sam couldn't help but laugh. It wasn't him... but he knew who the stench belonged to.

"You like to laugh, legionnaire?" said the aline. "I'll make you *scream*." He unsheathed a blade of his own, an ugly, black-stained piece of steel that looked more like a tooth than a knife. "Let's see, legionnaire, which of us succeeds in slicing the other's throat."

An otherworldly howl rose up over the sounds of blaster fire still echoing through the city.

The rebels looked around nervously. "What was that?"

"You don't want to know," Sam said, blood dripping from the corner of his mouth.

The aline sneered. "Time to die, Legionnaire."

"If I die, I'll do so thinking fondly of the look on your faces when she comes for you." Sam lifted his head to the sky. "I *do* need to talk to her about taking a bath, but beggars can't be choosers."

The aline waved the knife back and forth in the space between them, and Sam began to wonder whether this rebel actually wanted him dead, or was just playing mind games. If the roles were reversed, Sam would have already buried his blade up to the hilt in his opponent's eye.

He also wondered what was taking Fenra so long.

"I'm going to enjoy gutting you, Legionnaire." The aline studied Sam's armor as if searching for a spot to slide his knife through.

"So hurry up already," Sam grunted.

"Your pride is your downfall." The rebel drew back his arm to strike.

The next bloodcurdling howl sounded from the roof directly above the men.

CHAPTER 8

Fenra's eight-foot, five-hundred-plus-pound frame descended on the rebels like hell with fur and fangs. The rebel leader backpedaled out of her way, but not before he earned a swipe to remember her by. The lyconlore's razor-sharp claws drew bloody lines from his forehead to his chin, tearing the flesh from his face in ribbons. He screamed and fell backward, grabbing at his face as if he hoped to keep his nose and eyes intact by pressing them back into his skull.

As Fenra turned her attention to the other rebels, Sola appeared from the doorway with her blaster, and Colonel Minh raced down the alleyway with his squad. So much happened at once that Sam had to remind himself to get his hands on a weapon and join the fight. He fell to his knees, grabbed another of the sleek-looking rebel pistols, and opened fire.

The alley erupted in chaos, but the rebels didn't quit.

Fenra took a blaster bolt to the side as she lifted a rebel over her head and separated his body in two. Her howl of pain alerted Sola, who targeted the rebel responsible and took him out with a round right between the eyes.

It seemed like only seconds later that the rebels were down to two—one of whom was the aline, grabbing his face and leaving a trail of green blood. Somehow they escaped the kill zone and fled down the alley away from the colonel and his militia.

"We covered your six," Colonel Minh said, running up to Sam. He was practically jumping up and down; no doubt he felt his own adrenaline racing through his veins. "You hurt, Wolf? We'll fix you up good."

"I'm fine." Sam retrieved his helmet from the ground and put it back on. The L-comm was alive with chatter.

"Woohoo!" Bean was saying. "Light 'em up!"

"Get some!" Troy responded. "They're on the run, sir. They realized the Iron Wolves are in town, and they don't want *none* of what we're dishing out."

"Hold your position," said Captain Zeno. "You're not to give chase. Sergeant Samson, I see you're back online."

"Yes sir, I'm here now."

"Good. Almost had me worried. Report on your sweep."

"I think we have them on the run as well, Captain. We'll check the rest of the houses on this side to be sure and then link up with you in the center of the square."

"Roger that. Zeno out."

Sam turned to the colonel and his men. "You think you can clear the rest of the houses to be sure the rebels are really gone?"

"Sir, yes, sir," Colonel Minh said with a sharp salute. He was a colonel saluting a sergeant, but there was nothing but sincerity in the gesture. Even within the Republic armed forces, legionnaires, regardless of rank, managed to sit somewhat outside of the normal hierarchy.

Sam saluted back.

The colonel shouted orders to his men. "Okay, you heard the Wolf! Clear these buildings."

Sam turned his attention to Sola and Fenra. The former had rolled up her bandana and was tightening it around the wound on her leg. The latter was sitting in the dirt licking the fur on her side where the blaster had caught her.

That shot would have proved fatal to a human, but the big lyconlore, despite the pained look on her face, had hardly slowed down.

She saw Sam looking at her and growled something in her guttural tongue.

"We really need to work on your language," Sola said. "Where do you even learn these words?"

Fenra grunted and growled again.

"You are so lying. I've *never* used language like that, you shaggy piece of—" Sola stopped herself and shook her head. "Forget it. Doesn't matter. You deal with your own issues."

"What did she say?" Sam asked.

Sola scowled. "You don't want to know."

Fenra looked from Sola to Sam. She growled again, somewhat more intelligibly this time.

"She insists you owe her one." Sola limped over to Fenra to take a closer look at her wounds. "And she says you're one hell of a warrior. She was going to just let them gut you, but apparently she thought your crazy-man knife attack was 'inspiring.' She says you're not as weak as you look. *I* think you're an idiot, by the way."

"Great… I think," Sam said. He picked up another of the fallen alien blasters. The alley was littered with them—alongside alien corpses. "You know where they got these pistols? They look brand new."

Sola limped over and extended her hand, and he passed her the weapon.

"You two going to be all right?" he asked.

"We'll live." Sola turned the weapon over in her hands. "Though maybe we'll wish we hadn't. This weapon isn't one of ours, and it doesn't match what I've seen from any rebel faction in the north—and I've seen a lot of them."

"So, we've got an unknown supplier, or benefactor. Great." Sam took the weapon back, looked at it again, then studied the blaster on Sola's hip to see if it bore any resemblance.

"Hey, my eyes are up here." Sola crossed her arms and scowled. "I know you must be hurting for some vacation time but really, don't be an animal."

"What? Oh—no, I—" Sam was suddenly flustered. "I wasn't checking you out, really. Not at all. I mean, not that I don't think you're… well…" Sam stopped himself. Why had he even started that sentence?

"Keep going." Sola's scowl turned to amusement in the space of a second. "What were you going to say?"

"Nothing." Sam shook his head. "I was just checking to see if your blaster resembled the rebel pistol. That's all. Calm yourself."

Sola drew her weapon and extended it grip-first to Sam. The move took her a fraction of a second.

"Look for yourself," she said. "It's a Reaper 210. I modified the trigger and tweaked the sights, but that's about it."

Sam had heard of the Reaper 210—in stories of the Savage Wars. This was a weapon he'd expect to see in a museum, not on the field of battle.

He tested the fierce hand cannon in his grip. It felt amazing, like a pistol version of a club or mace. "Where did you get this?"

Before she could answer, Minh and his team reappeared. "All clear, Iron Wolf," he said. "We ran the rebel scum from the city, thanks to you and the legionnaires!"

Fenra bared her teeth at the colonel.

The colonel quickly added, "And of course with the help of Fenra and Sola." He swallowed hard. "The rest of my men are gathering at the town center now. What should we do?"

Sam handed the Reaper back to Sola, making a mental note to revisit the discussion of the weapon sometime in the near future.

"Hold that thought," he said to the colonel. He opened a comm channel to Captain Zeno. "Captain, we're confirmed clear on this side of the square. Orders?"

Zeno's voice carried a hint of wonder, the likes of which he had never heard before from the man. "Sergeant, we've found something over here. Bring the guide and the Conongan CO you've been working with. We need to figure out what we're dealing with."

CHAPTER 9

"Colonel Minh," Sam said, "set up a perimeter and secure the city, then report personally to the town square."

"Yes, right away." Colonel Minh gave another crisp salute that bordered on comical, despite his very serious features. He turned to his men and began doling out orders.

Sam turned to Sola. "Sola and Fenra, if you would come with me, they've found something on the other side of the square."

The three of them moved out of the alley, Sola limping, Fenra bringing up the rear. Years of experience made Sam check and double-check the rooftops and spaces between the buildings as they crossed the open square to the copse of greenery at its center.

Sola clearly noticed. "You can take it easy, Legionnaire. They're all dead or fled." She threw a thumb behind her at Fenra. "Fenra would be able to smell them if they were still here."

Sam just nodded. Assuring as that might be, his vigilance in checking windows and doorways was involuntary.

Besides, the big gal didn't sniff the rebels out *before* the shooting started.

The town square was littered with the bodies of not only rebels, but civilians caught in the crossfire. The enemy corpses were easy to deal with. His eyes just scanned them to make sure they were actually dead. KTF those kelhorns.

When he looked at a civilian body though, clothing choked with blood, insides hanging out like hoses from a machine... he turned away and forced himself to think of something else. He had witnessed this sort of scene dozens of times before. The ugly truth was, innocent people died in war zones every day, but even though he was a man of violence, a man prone to blinding rage, he would never be numbed to the death of civilians.

In a strange way, he felt good about that. Like it proved he still had an ember of decency and civility glowing beneath his Legion-chiseled exterior.

They were nearly to the middle of the square when Sam spotted a body that hit him harder than the rest. He was just a boy. The very same wide-eyed boy who had eagerly stopped him to ask if he was really an Iron Wolf.

Sam stopped at the boy's side. Forced himself to look.

A blaster round had struck the child on the side of his face. The impact was so violent, it looked to have broken his neck. Sam pictured the poor kid spinning around a full one hundred and eighty degrees before hitting the dirt.

He saw it as clearly as if he were watching a movie.

His mind wouldn't let him see anything else.

Emptiness touched him. He should be sad for this boy. Angry for this boy. But he felt... cold.

What had the boy done to deserve this? This... *child*... had woken up this morning excited to see the Iron Wolves, and he would never wake up again. His life had been snuffed out like it was nothing.

Why him? Why not me?

It's the universe we live in.

Sam took a deep breath. He had to bury this down deep, nice and healthy like. He had a job to do right now. He had to make sure this didn't happen to any other kids. Not if he could help it.

"The universe is an ugly place." Sola had come to stand beside him. "Just plain bad luck. He was at the wrong place at the wrong time."

"Luck had nothing to do with it." Sam forced his gaze away from the boy's still body. "Men made conscious decisions that led to this boy's death. Now it's *our* turn to make decisions. Decisions that lead those men to their graves."

He walked off without waiting for a response.

Captain Zeno stood beside the central copse with Doc Dobson and Private Moon. All three had their helmets removed, and they were talking in hushed tones.

"Sergeant," Captain Zeno said as Sam approached. He eyed Sam's limp, then Sola's, and finally squinted at the cracked and blistered wound in Fenra's gray coat. "Looks like it didn't go as smooth as you suggested over the comms. Do you need medical attention?"

"Not personally, sir." Sam ignored Doc Dobson's questioning eyes. "Sola and Fenra might need a quick look though." He removed his helmet, forgetting the damage the rebel leader's strikes had done to his face.

"Sarge… you don't look fine," Private Moon said with a raised eyebrow. "You sure you okay?"

"I said I'm good." Sam spoke more harshly than he meant to. As Doc stepped forward to inspect Sola's and Fenra's wounds, Sam quickly changed the subject. "How did clearing the buildings on your side of the square go?"

"Nine Wolves went into the battle, nine still on their feet," Captain Zeno said. "Troy has a mild concussion and Bean took a few rounds to his armor, but the worst he'll have is some nasty bruises. This new armor can turn a blaster round away like it's nothing. It'd be nice to get replacements like this more often. Gear like this would save a lot of lives on the front lines."

"Guess it's more important to save it for PR stunts, when they want us to play dress-up for the Senate," Sam grumbled. "So we just trudge around in stuff that's barely holding together. What a joke."

"You got that right." Captain Zeno rolled his shoulder. "But we have bigger rebels to fry at the moment. We found something while we were clearing out our side of the square. Something that had no business being there." He tilted his head toward Moon. "Even our resident tech-head here doesn't know what to make of it."

"You gonna tell me what it is, sir?" Sam asked. His mind was racing with possibilities.

"We'll show you." Captain Zeno looked over to Doc. "You good here? They going to be okay?"

"Roger that, sir." Doc Dobson had Sola and Fenra sitting next to one another. He was rubbing his nose due to the lyconlore's odor. "I'll have them patched up in no time."

"Then let's go."

The captain led Sam and Moon to a hut, crudely built out of mismatched boards, not far from a row of houses and shops. "In here. I had the rest of the unit set up a perimeter around... around whatever it is."

The tone in the captain's voice was more than enough to make Sam worry. Anything that gave Captain Zeno pause was pretty serious.

Troy stood guard outside the hut's wooden door. He saluted the approaching legionnaires. "Moony!" he yelled. "All good here, safe and secure!"

"Quiet down, man, you're yelling," Moon said. He looked over at Sam and explained, "Troy was a bit too close to a shock grenade. He'll be fine, just... he can't hear sket for a while."

"What?" Troy screamed. "Who's yellowing? Someone puking it all up?"

"Put your bucket on, Legionnaire," Captain Zeno growled.

He moved past Troy into the building, while Troy fumbled to obey. He heard *that* much at least.

Sam and Moon followed the captain into a wide open space that seemed to be a living room, kitchen, dining area, and bedroom all in one. The place was an ordinary pauper's home, just what you'd expect on a planet like Cononga. Dirt floors underfoot, a chipped table, some dingy dishes stacked behind the sink...

And then there was the strange object.

In the middle of the living area sat a metallic cylinder with a wide base and six legs for support. It gave off an ever so slight, high-pitched whine, barely audible even with bucket-enhancing audio. Resting on top of the cylinder was a vial of blue liquid.

"I, uh… if you think I can help you identify this thing, sir," said Sam, "I'm afraid I have no idea. But it doesn't belong in this hovel, that's for damn sure."

"No, it doesn't," said Zeno. "And whatever it is, we know it was important to the rebels, because the men guarding this building didn't retreat when everyone else did. We had to put them down." He nodded at Moon. "The private here has a working theory. Moon?"

Moon walked around the contraption. "I haven't seen this kind of setup before, but I believe its function is to turn that blue liquid into a gas and then deliver it into the air. The liquid lowers into the machine—you can see the valve there—and then you see these ports? Kind of like sprayers? Safe to say they're gonna, you know, spray. I'll need to do some tests on the liquid, but this is either the strangest room deodorizer I've ever seen, or…" He raised his eyebrows.

"You're talking about chemical warfare." Sam heard his own voice go an octave lower. "The rebels planned to gas the city?"

"That's what it looks like," Moon said. "Again, I need to test the liquid to be sure."

Sam looked over to the captain. "What did we walk into?"

"I don't know." Captain Zeno's one good eye narrowed. "But I'm gonna get some answers."

At that moment a sweating Colonel Minh entered the building. He gave a sharp salute to each of the legionnaires in turn, including Private Moon. "Sirs, the city is being secured as we speak. What are we to do next?"

"Captain Zeno, this is Colonel Minh," Sam said. "Colonel, this is our commander, Captain Zeno."

Colonel Minh saluted yet again, this time even more crisply, if that was possible.

Captain Zeno's eye twinkled with amusement as he returned the salute. "Good to meet you, Colonel. Thank you for mobilizing and aiding us in clearing the square."

"Of course." Colonel Minh peered around the captain to the metal contraption. "It is my life's honor to serve next to the Iron Wolves. How may I assist you further?"

"I'm glad you asked." Captain Zeno gave the man a stare that made the colonel swallow audibly. "We need to talk to the president."

CHAPTER 10

Sam and the captain were left waiting in a side room on the second story of the presidential palace. The building was far from gaudy, but Sam got the feeling that, by Conongan standards, it was elaborately decorated.

Purple blinds against large windows filtered the soft light that fell on simple purple couches and chairs. Plants in massive pots stood sentry in the corners of the room, and a golden chandelier hung from the ceiling. Through the blinds was a view of the palace grounds and the city beyond.

Sam joined Captain Zeno, who was looking out into the city of Noi. Now that the conflict was over, the people were coming back. Wails of sorrow for loved ones caught in the crossfire could be heard on the still air.

Lyn entered the room behind them. "Ah, gentlemen, I am so glad you were unharmed in that, uh... unpleasantness. You realize I wanted to help, but I'm a noncombatant..." He shook his head from side to side like a little kid who didn't want to eat his vegetables.

"That's not what we're here to talk about," Sam said. He had no patience for the Senate liaison right now. The aches in his face and leg were throbbing now that his adrenaline had worn off. "We need an audience with the president."

"Colonel Minh said that wouldn't be a problem," Zeno added.

"Oh. Why yes, of course." Lyn nodded furiously. "I'll go and get him right away. And I'll see that your men are provided with a hot meal and quarters as well. Do you two need food, or showers, or—"

"When we're done here," Captain Zeno said, interrupting. "Answers come first. Blood was spilled today, and I *will* know why before I wash said blood off my armor. You get me?"

"Understood," Lyn squeaked. "I'll only be a moment." He scurried out the door.

"You know this isn't a coincidence," Captain Zeno said, returning his gaze to the city. "I mean, past your belief in Oba and all that. It's not a roll of the dice that made the rebels attack today of all days."

"I know," Sam said. "This was a coordinated attack—it took a lot of planning. And if that chemical weapon had detonated"—Sam didn't need to wait for Moon's tests; he was sure that's what it was—"who knows what the death toll would have been." He turned to face the captain. "You think our helmets would have protected us?"

"I don't know." Captain Zeno shrugged. "Supposed to, but it probably depends on the gas. We'll have to see if we can find a lab, or whatever they have here that will pass for a lab, and get Moon to work. And Sam… please don't start with the mumbo-jumbo now. I'm in no mood."

"Sir?"

"You know what I mean. The whole 'everything happens for a reason' speech. How Oba brought us here to help these people and all that. You know I don't believe that."

"Just because you don't believe it doesn't mean it's not true," Sam said, pushing the subject ever so slightly. "Sir."

Sam had been with the captain for two years. During that time he'd been a sergeant slightly more often than he'd been a corporal—his rank fluctuating due to his... enthusiasm about combat. And while he wouldn't call the man a friend, he *would* call him a brother. In a heartbeat. It didn't matter one whit that the two men didn't share the same religious beliefs—at all. Sam trusted this man with his life. The captain was an amazing legionnaire and an even better leader.

"I've seen too many good men die, for no reason at all, to ever believe there's some master plan to all this," Captain Zeno said, shaking his head as if he were seeing the memories before him. "And I say 'men,' but most of them were just kids. Boys sent by the House of Reason and Senate to die on foreign soil for private agendas. The kind of wars that serve only to line the pockets of cowards too spineless to ever pick up a weapon on their own."

Sam didn't disagree, but this was the sort of talk one had to be careful with. At least when there were points around. So even though Major Roy was miles out of earshot, Sam said only, "Yes, sir."

It wasn't enough. *You've got to say something more,* Sam thought. *This is the most he's ever talked to you about this. Say something. Ugh, you're going to think of the perfect thing to say, in the next few hours when it's too late.*

"Maybe that's exactly why I have to believe in a bigger plan," he said. It was the first thing that came to his mind. "I've seen my brothers die beside me, and if this is all for nothing—if nothing we do *means* anything—then why do we keep doing it? Why do we keep fighting? Dying?"

Captain Zeno was about to reply when Lyn returned with President Gen.

"My apologies for keeping you men waiting," the president said. He motioned toward the overstuffed sofas. "Please, sit. We have much to discuss."

"I hope no offense will be taken if I stand." Captain Zeno bowed his head slightly to show he meant no disrespect.

President Gen waved away the thought magnanimously. "Of course."

"I'd like for you to tell me a story, sir," Zeno said. "A story that starts with where these rebels came from and why they're carrying brand-new weapons and technology. End the story—if you can—with why we were all ambushed today."

Sam was taken aback. He hadn't expected Zeno to bow with reverence, but neither had he ever imagined his CO would speak to the president with a tone bordering on interrogation.

"Captain, please," Lyn said, rising from his couch. He was the only one who had taken a seat. "President Gen must be addressed with—"

"It's fine." President Gen smoothed down the white fabric of his robe over his ample belly. "I feel the same eagerness to get everyone on the same page and find answers to the holes in a story I am unable to fill myself."

Lyn licked his lips and nodded. He seemed relieved. Slightly.

"The rebels to the north have never been a problem," the president began. "At least, never like this. They started years ago as a small band of protesters preaching a communist dictatorship and the overthrow of my government. *Our* government. Cononga is ruled by the people. Over time, the northern rebels have grown in numbers, thanks largely to promising things they can never possibly deliver. But until now, they've done nothing more than protest—and maybe do a little minor harassment here and there. Never have they attacked us outright. I could never have imagined they were even capable of what they did today."

"And their weapons?" Captain Zeno said. "Where would they have gotten shiny new rifles and chemical assets like the ones we recovered today?"

"I have no hard facts. Only guesses." The president looked troubled, as if by voicing the words he was realizing their meaning for the first time. "The planet of Cononga is not like many of your Republic worlds. We are far from united. One planet, yes, but with many countries, many governments. And some of those countries, including our neighbors to the north, are strongly opposed to Cononga's entrance into the Republic, because it will only be a matter of time before the entire planet joins. They know this. I know this. I believe it is they who are equipping the rebels."

Sam remembered the aline in the alley. "These neighbors to the north..." he said. "Are they a different species?"

President Gen took in a deep lungful of air, and released it. "Yes, that's right."

"I may have run into one today. He was a chatty character, about my build, green skin, bald head, a dangle of lips over his teeth. An aline, I thought, but they're not native to Cononga."

"This is correct. A colony of alines settled in the north during the Savage Wars, seeking to escape their own world, which, as I understand it, was ruined by the Savages. If you saw one of them with the attackers today... then I consider it confirmed. The rebels are receiving weapons from the alines. Judging by their tactics today, I assume they're getting military training, too. They're clearly a threat like never before." He looked earnestly at Zeno. "We are now part of the Republic, though. They will help us, yes?"

The president's face looked so pathetic, so innocent. So naïve. This man was new to the modern dealings of the Republic. It wasn't as simple as an ally needing help and the Republic coming to the rescue. In the Savage Wars, things were different. If a planet needed help, the Legion came running, but those days died long ago.

The president looked from Zeno to Sam. Though neither had said a word, he must have read the doubt in their expressions.

"Maybe just the Iron Wolves?" he said hopefully. "Yes, maybe the great Iron Wolves will be enough."

Captain Zeno crossed his arms and asked a question Sam had been wondering ever since they'd landed. No, since before that. Since they were first assigned to this mission.

"I've done my fair share of killing," Zeno said, "and you can be sure the Iron Wolves are a force to be reckoned with. It's... unusual that we should be called on for a diplomatic mission, such as this one was meant to be. President Gen... why did you specifically request the Iron Wolves for this ceremony? And why do you talk about us like you know us?"

President Gen looked confused. He turned to Lyn. "They weren't told?"

"I—uh, I wasn't exactly sure myself." Lyn said, squirming. "I thought you had heard of their exploits and chose them based on that."

President Gen turned away sharply. "Please, follow me."

He marched out of the chamber like a man on a mission, without waiting to see if anyone was accompanying him.

Lyn jogged to catch up.

Sam looked to his captain for instruction. Zeno nodded, and the two legionnaires followed.

The palace halls were carpeted in cream, making a slight contrast with the crisp white walls. Floor-to-ceiling windows made the place look larger than it was—but those windows would make the palace a nightmare to defend, if it came to that.

The president led them down two flights of stairs to the basement level, then through two more hallways. He stopped at a pair of wooden doors and pulled out a key that hung on a necklace buried in his white robes. With a practiced motion, he placed the key in the lock and turned the deadbolt.

Sam was suddenly and painfully aware that they had brought no weapons into the palace. He didn't have so much as a knife to use if this was some kind of trap. Then again, if it was a trap, a knife wouldn't save the two legionnaires.

You're being paranoid, Sam.

President Gen opened the double doors and stepped through.

"If things go bad here," Captain Zeno whispered, as if he were reading Sam's thoughts, "this looks like a good spot for a last stand. And try to loosen up, Sergeant."

"Roger that, sir." But every muscle in Sam's body tensed as they walked into the chamber. He felt ready for anything.

He wasn't.

CHAPTER 11

The doors led into a long hall that looked like a museum. Neither Sam nor the captain said a word as they soaked in the scene.

Weapons were mounted on the walls and set on display stands. *Ancient* weapons. Blasters, blades, cudgels. Tech from the very beginning of the Savage Wars. Tapestries were interspersed with the weapons. Most featured images of heroic legionnaires and Conongan soldiers, fighting together against Savage marines pouring from their great lighthuggers. Glass cases featured medals—also from the Savage Wars era—and framed pictures of grizzled legionnaires standing shoulder to shoulder with Conongan soldiers.

Almost all of the legionnaires had the Iron Wolf emblem on their armor.

President Gen stood on a raised platform at the other end of the hall, patiently waiting for them. "You understand now," he said, "why my people hold the Iron Wolves in such high regard."

The two legionnaires and an open-mouthed Lyn joined President Gen on the platform. He stood beside an aged, torn flag that had been stained with blood and battle. An early Iron Wolf flag, with the familiar snarling wolf's head in the center.

"My ancestors fought the Savages here on Cononga, with the Iron Wolves at our side," the president said. "Stories of those legendary battles have been passed down from generation to generation."

Lyn's mouth hung open even wider. Sam found himself staring at a piece of green smashed between two of the man's molars.

"Your unit have been heroes to us ever since," the president continued. "My father and grandfather spent long nights telling how the Iron Wolves bravely led my people into battle. That is why you, specifically, were requested here today. I could imagine no other unit but the Iron Wolves standing with us on our day of entering the Republic. My people look to you as legends."

Sam didn't know what to say. At least he hid his astonishment better than the Senate liaison.

"You can close your mouth now," Captain Zeno said to Lyn. "You're starting to drool."

Lyn snapped his jaw shut.

"I would have shared these stories at the ceremony, had we not been interrupted by the rebel attack," President Gen said. "I told the Senate all of this, of course, but perhaps they forgot to mention it to you."

"The Senate and the House of Reason both do a lot of forgetting these days," Captain Zeno said.

He gave Lyn a hard stare. "So what happens now, Mr. Nix? Is the Republic ready to help Cononga?"

The Senate liaison wouldn't meet Zeno's eye. "Yes, about that." He coughed into his hand. "I was—I was on the comm with Major Roy while you were repelling the rebels. He said, uh..." He took a deep breath, then said quickly, as if to get it over with, "He said we were to cease all negotiations with the nation of Cononga until he had the opportunity to relay the events and receive orders from the House of Reason."

President Gen beamed. "Ah! So it is just a matter of formalities before our allies in the Republic will assist us. Good. With the Iron Wolves and our militia—limited though it may be—we will surely be able to hold out until then."

Lyn looked down, his face flushing. "One can only hope..."

Sam felt his stomach twist. He'd heard Lyn just as clearly as the president had, but he recognized carefully chosen weasel words when he heard them. *Politics.*

Apparently, Captain Zeno heard the same thing—and was far less sanguine about it. He grabbed Lyn around the throat and slammed him against the wall. "Give it to him straight, you coward." His voice was cold. "Look into the president's eyes and tell him, plainly, that we're going to leave him now. Tell him that since he has not yet signed the treaty allying his people with the Republic, the Senate will use that as a convenient excuse to abandon them. Tell him that right now, when they most need our help, we're going to leave them."

Sam agreed with every word coming out of the captain's mouth. Anger welled in his chest. Anger for every time he'd been forced to leave a battle that was actually worth fighting for. Anger for every time he'd been forced to fight a battle that would do nothing but line the pockets of the corrupt.

But he couldn't just stand here while the captain strangled Lyn. The man's face was turning blue.

He placed a hand on the captain's shoulder. He didn't dare speak. Not when the man's ire was up. He just put his hand there. Gently.

Captain Zeno shook with rage under Sam's touch.

"Captain…"

Finally Zeno loosened his grip, prompting a sputtering of coughs as color returned to Lyn's face. The Senate liaison dropped to his knees.

"I—I'm sorry, Captain. But—it's the way things work." Lyn rubbed his throat. "Please—try and understand…"

"So then it's the worst possible scenario." President Gen's voice was sad and distant. "The Republic will turn their backs on us. Even the Iron Wolves… Even our legends will not stand with us. And now that the rebels have the backing of the alines…" He turned away. "We'll be slaughtered."

"I'm sorry—I'm sorry," Lyn said. He rose to his feet, regaining his composure. "Sir, my orders are clear. We're to stand down. We are not to interfere with the civil war you have going on here. And if things are not resolved in the space of a few days, we're to pull out and return to the *Breaker.*"

"We were so close," President Gen said. He turned to face them once more, and his face held a look of twisted remorse. "We were one day away from signing the treaty with the Republic. For years we have dreamed of this..."

Sam wanted to spit again. He wanted to grab one of the ancient weapons from the wall and take it right into the Senate. And then take it to the rebels for good measure.

"Don't give up yet," Captain Zeno said. He was still glaring at Lyn. "I'm going to contact Major Roy one more time. Maybe there's something to be done."

"Thank you, Captain," President Gen pressed his hands together like he was saying a prayer, and bowed.

"Don't thank me yet." Captain Zeno turned to leave, and motioned for Sam to follow. "Lyn, I'm using your comm to communicate with the *Breaker*."

"Of course." Lyn hurried in front of the men to show them the way. He seemed eager to please the man who'd nearly choked him out. "I—really am so sorry. I wish there were more I could do, but I'm only a representative. I follow orders, just like you."

"You're nothing like us," Captain Zeno growled.

"Honestly, Captain Zeno," Lyn said in a small voice— and no wonder, the captain sounded more like an animal than a man—"I'd appreciate an apology at this point. I would gladly accept. I understand we are all operating in a stressed environment, and I want you to know that I don't plan on filing a formal report on you."

Sam couldn't help but be slightly impressed at the man's boldness. It was the first sign that the liaison had an actual spine.

"*What* did you just say?" Captain Zeno looked like he was going to reach inside Lyn and snap that spine in two.

"Lyn," Sam said, interrupting before things could escalate further. "Save it. Let's look forward rather than back, shall we?"

Lyn nodded. "Of course, Sergeant."

"Now. Hypothetically speaking," Sam asked, "if the rebels had attacked tomorrow instead of today—*after* the treaty had been signed—would we still be ordered out of here, or would we be calling in reinforcements right now?"

"If the president had already signed the treaty, we would have some obligation to provide aid, of course," Lyn said with a heavy sigh. "But we have our orders."

"So have the president sign the damned thing and say it's done," snapped Captain Zeno.

"It's not that easy, sir. They already know."

Lyn quickly led the men back up to the first floor of the palace, to a small room furnished with nothing but a single table and chair. A comm sat on the table.

"You two still look like you want to hurt me," Lyn said, "so I'm going to leave you. But you must be starving. I'll have food sent to you." The Senate liaison bowed out of the room.

"Thank you," Sam said to the man's back. He wanted to believe that Lyn was just an idiot caught up in events, rather than a conniving Senate puppet.

"You want some privacy, sir?" Sam asked as Zeno placed his helmet on the table and tuned the comm. "I can step outside."

"No. I need you here as a witness to what is about to be said." He looked up at Sam. "But you'd better close the door."

CHAPTER 12

Captain Zeno waited for a response over the digital hum of the comm.

Major Roy came online sounding indifferent and bored. "Go ahead, Captain Zeno. What is your status?"

"The unit is secure in the palace awaiting orders, sir, but our allies down here are facing issues with their neighbors to the north. I'm requesting permission to aid them until—"

"That's a negative, Captain," Major Roy said. "I received information that they are not, in fact, our allies as of yet—and should not be treated as such. I've been in direct contact with the Senate on this. You are ordered to stand down and remain a neutral party. I will leave you on planet for the time being, so that if the situation resolves itself quickly, we can move forward with the treaty. But if this conflict appears to be an ongoing concern, I'll be sending a shuttle to evacuate you and your unit."

"Sir, that would mean we'd be turning our backs on these people right when they need us the most." Captain Zeno looked at Sam and pulled his lips back from his teeth, indicating how hard he was working to contain his anger.

"There's a *very* small band of rebels harassing them, with aid from their enemies to the north. We could provide you with coordinates. A few well-placed orbital strikes from the *Breaker*, and we can have this resolved in the space of twenty-four hours."

Major Roy gave a heavy sigh that suggested he was tired of going round with Zeno about this. "That's a negative, Captain Zeno. The Senate won't risk any strikes; it would throw us into a war. You're suggesting we initiate a conflict in order to protect a country that, I remind you once more, is *not* our ally. And if allying with that country is expected to provide the Republic with more cost than benefit, as it now appears is the case, we're to pull out of the agreement. Do you understand?"

"Yes, sir." Captain Zeno relaxed like a man who had accepted his fate. "I understand loud and clear, sir."

"Good. In three days, you are to report back in with the status of the Cononga. If nothing has changed, you'll be pulled out." Major Roy finished his thought with a sniff. "Over."

"Over."

Captain Zeno turned off the comm and drummed his fingers on the table. His calm nature sent a shiver down Sam's spine. He couldn't help but feel like the captain was going to snap.

"We're not going to stand down, are we, sir?" Sam asked.

"*I'm* not going to stand down." Captain Zeno looked Sam in the eye. "But I have no intention of obligating you or the others to join me. You heard our orders. I'm going to relay those orders to the men, then allow them to decide for themselves… and face the repercussions."

"Sir, I think you know the men will follow your lead. What precisely do you plan to do?"

Zeno stood from his seat. "I'm going to take it to these rebels and their allies. I'm going to show them what trying to kill kids and families with chemical warfare gets them: two to the body and one to the head."

Lyn appeared in the doorway with a loaded platter of food. "Who's hungry?" he said in a pleasant, singsong way, as though the captain hadn't nearly choked him to death thirty minutes earlier. Maybe ignoring slights—and outright assaults—was a necessary character trait for surviving the corridors of the House of Reason and Senate. "I've got sandwiches," he sang.

Captain Zeno grabbed two pieces of flat bread on either side of a mass of unidentifiable meat.

Sam absentmindedly accepted a sandwich as well. He was still thinking about what the captain had said. He was going to go rogue. The rest of the men would likely follow him. The question was… what would Sam do?

You already know what you're going to do. You're just kidding yourself if you even pretend to take the time to think about it.

Sam bit into the sandwich. It was good: some kind of spiced meat mixed with a combination of mustard and vinegar. His stomach growled with appreciation, and he quickly devoured the rest. He noted Zeno doing the same.

"Well then, maybe we can all have a nice chat now that you both have some food in your stomachs," Lyn said, pouring glasses of a yellow liquid. "Or perhaps you'd like a hot shower first? Quarters have been prepared for you both, and clean clothes as well."

"Why aren't you eating too?" Captain Zeno asked as he reached for another sandwich. "You didn't poison this food, did you?"

Lyn's face went pale. "I—no, I would never." He grabbed a sandwich from the platter, took a large bite, and washed it down with a gulp of the yellow liquid. "See? No poison. No need to choke me again, Captain."

Captain Zeno eyed the Senate liaison suspiciously as he reached for his glass. Sam was pretty sure the captain was just messing with Lyn... but given what had happened earlier, he couldn't be entirely sure.

"What is this anyway?" Sam asked, tasting the yellow liquid. "It tastes a little like citrus and... and something else I can't place."

"Oh, it's a delicacy here. It's called Bullvine, made from the urine of a yamsach," Lyn said matter-of-factly.

Sam spewed the Bullvine from his mouth all over the floor. "Did you just say *urine*?" Out of the corner of his eye he saw the captain crack a rare grin.

"That's right. It's good, though." Lyn looked at Sam as if he were crazy. "It's guaranteed to clean you right out in the next few hours."

"Yeah, I think I'll pass." Sam put his glass back on the tray and grabbed another sandwich.

"Better make that sandwich to go, Sergeant," Zeno said. "I'd like to go see the rest of the unit. I have a question for them."

"Of course. I'll take you to them," Lyn said.

As Sam followed, chewing his sandwich, he felt a strange sense of calm. Some sket was about to hit the fan, that was for damn sure, but at least now he knew what was going on, and that made all the difference. A short while ago he couldn't even have said where the fan was.

They heard the rest of their unit before they saw them.

"Are you racisizing against me?" Bean was saying.

Troy broke out laughing. "That's not even a word. And there's no such thing among leejes. Blue, purple, green or yellow, you know you're my brother from another mother."

"I still think you're kind of racist," Bean said jokingly. "I mean you just finished saying you only dream in black and white."

Sam, Lyn, and Zeno came to the open door where the two men were bunking for the night. The two privates immediately stopped their banter and jumped to attention. Both men were dressed in the synthprene bodysuits they had worn under their armor. There was an empty platter of food on a table, and wet towels indicated they'd already had a chance to shower.

"Sir!" they shouted as one.

"At ease." Captain Zeno motioned to the clean armor that sat at the foot of their beds. "I see you've been busy. I need you to follow me. We need to talk."

"Yes, sir!"

Sam walked down the hall past the other open doors where his men had been quartered. "Iron Wolves, let's go! It's time to turn the wheels of the future."

With a rustling of boots and bodies, the eight Iron Wolves readied themselves and joined the sergeant and the captain in the hall.

All eyes turned expectantly to Lyn. He nodded and smiled amiably, and even waved at a few of the men, as if greeting old friends.

Sam raised an eyebrow and motioned down the hall with his thumb.

"Oh? Oh! Yes of course," Lyn said, backing away. "You go ahead and speak in private. And there's an exit just down the hall that will take you out into a back courtyard if you need more privacy."

"Wolves on me," Zeno said. He headed the opposite way down the hall and found the door leading out into the open air.

Almost everyone was quiet, the exceptions being the incorrigible Bean and Troy, who were whispering something between themselves. For Sam, the seriousness of the moment pressed on him like a weight-training vest during a ten-click hump. Although the other men were still in the dark about the situation, he suspected they felt the same.

The door led to a courtyard, as Lyn had promised. Cononga's sun had descended out of sight behind the surrounding buildings, and the afternoon heat had given way to a pleasant evening warmth. The captain stopped beside a curved stone bench that was enclosed in a circle of shrubbery.

Even Bean and Troy were quiet now. If hiding out in a palace courtyard wasn't clue enough, the intensity in Captain Zeno's eye made it clear to everyone... that now was the time to listen.

CHAPTER 13

"You men know me well," Captain Zeno began. "You know I'm a legionnaire first and forever. And you... you're not only my men—you're my family. My brothers. As such, I'm going to tell you everything I know about what's going on on this planet. Then you'll each be free to make your own decision as to how you'd like to proceed."

Sam stood next to Doc Dobson who seemed to straighten himself even more than usual. Sam guessed the rest of the men had similar stances; he was too focused on the captain to look down the line.

Captain Zeno stalked back and forth in front of his men. The gray and white in his dark hair caught the sun's setting rays. "Major Roy has ordered us to stand down," he said. "Those orders were relayed to him directly from the Senate. We're to remain neutral, stay out of the conflict here, and wait a few days to see if the rebels and the Conongans can sort this all out. If the situation is not resolved soon, however, we are to leave the planet.

"Now, I don't know about you, but I've left *enough* fights. I don't know if there can ever be absolution for me and the things I've done. Probably not. So I concern myself with the here and now. So, here's what I know about the rebels who started that firefight in the square. They could not have cared less about the collateral damage they caused. They had no regard for the innocent people—including children—who were caught in the crossfire, and I'll tell you why they didn't care: because they *intended* to kill them all. We uncovered, in their possession, what I'm confident is a chemical weapon meant to wipe out the entire city."

The captain looked over to Private Moon. "Moon, did you get an opportunity to test the substance?"

"I did, sir." Private Moon looked down the line. "It's a neurotoxin. Messes with the brain's ability to do a number of things—including breathing. Anyone affected by this chemical would be unable to take a breath until they blacked out and died. They'd be aware of this the entire time."

Captain Zeno halted his pacing in front of Sam. "These rebels, and the nation to the north that's backing them, intended to inflict that fate on an entire city of innocent people. They would have done so today had we not been here. They may do so tomorrow if we leave."

He looked over his men. "Orders or no orders, I'm not going anywhere. I'm staying. I'm fighting."

He fell silent. He was asking the men to make their own decisions now. To join him, and face the consequences, or to follow orders. He didn't need to put that question into words. Everyone knew.

"All due respect, Captain," Thompson said, stroking his thick beard, "you lead anywhere and you know I'll follow. But if this isn't sanctioned by the powers that be, is it worth sticking our necks out for? I mean, let's say we go rogue, slaughter some rebels and send them packing. What's to say they won't just start things up again the moment we leave this planet?"

Captain Zeno nodded along as the legionnaire spoke. "I've thought about that," he said. "And under normal circumstances, I'd agree, but we have a special situation here. According to the information we've received from the Senate, if we suppress the rebels quickly enough, if we can convince the Republic that the situation on Cononga is under control, the treaty will still move forward. Once that happens, Cononga will be protected by the Republic. The rebels will know that, and that's a damn powerful deterrent."

Silence fell again as every man thought on his choice.

Captain Zeno started his pacing again. "I can't, nor would I, command you to go against orders from our superiors. All I can do is lay out the facts and tell you what I plan to do. If any of you would rather sit this one out, I'm the last person that should judge. I've sat out plenty in my time."

"Did you regret it, sir?" Sam asked, his heart beating like a hammer in his chest. "When you sat on the sideline?"

"Every day," Captain Zeno growled. He swallowed hard as if all the memories washed over him at once. "Every damn day, Sergeant."

Sam considered the repercussions of going rogue. Worst case, they would be killed by the rebels. Best case, they would be disciplined by their superiors and kicked out of the Legion.

On second thought, maybe getting killed by rebels was the better option.

The images of the boy in the square flashed through Sam's mind. He knew it was a sight he would never forget.

He nodded once. "I'm with you, sir." He stepped forward to stand beside the captain. "If we have a chance to do some good, I'm going to do it. I'm not going to sit in a campsite a few clicks from here and eat breakfast while this place burns."

Troy stretched his arms and walked to stand next to his two superiors. "Well, I just checked in with my private secretary, and it appears I can make some time on my calendar for the next day or two. We're going to need some supplies, though. My N-4 ran dry during that last engagement."

"I'm in," Private Moon and Doc Dobson said at almost the same time. They came forward to stand with the others.

But when Bean stepped forward, Troy held up a hand to stop him. "Listen, brother, there's no one I'd rather have beside me in a fight, but you got a family to think about back home. Don't put them second just because you feel you have to. We won't think any less of you."

"They're *why* I have to," Bean said. "I'm not going back home, looking them in the eye, and telling them I ran. I'm going to be the man they think I am."

In the next few seconds everyone had joined the captain. Except Thompson. The unit's sniper sighed heavily and tapped his boot on the ground. Everyone waited for him to make his decision.

Finally, he spoke. "Oh, I'm with you, you know. I'm gonna do the whole walk over to your side of the line and all. I'm just soaking in a few more seconds of being sane first."

"Sanity's overrated," Sam said with a grin. "Besides, none of us were sane to begin with. We're legionnaires. We signed up for this."

Laughter broke out among the men, and Thompson grinned as he came to stand with them.

"So what's the plan?" Doc Dobson asked. He looked from Sam to the captain. "We've got no intel, we're out of charge packs, and we're way outmanned."

The men quieted.

"I agree with your assessment. So let's start planning." Captain Zeno turned his head and called, "You can come out now! We're finished."

Sam turned to see Sola walking around the corner of the shrubbery. There was still a hitch in her step from her wound, but she was as tough as they came.

"I wanted to be respectful and give you boys your moment and all that," Sola said, as if she had been expecting to be called out. "If you're open to suggestions, I might have a few ideas."

"I'm all ears," Captain Zeno said.

She smiled. "Intel I can handle. Fenra and I know where the rebels stay encamped in the jungle. Most times. And if not, we can always go and see what's what. Fenra is a lot stealthier than she looks. Weapons... that's a bigger problem. I'd suggest we make use of the blasters the rebels dropped, but the militia took all those almost as quickly as they hit the ground. And frankly, they need those guns as bad as you do. Odd as it sounds, your best bet may be to salvage what you can from the president's Savage Wars museum."

The men exchanged a few confused—and concerned—glances. They didn't know about the museum yet. Sam would have to reassure them later. If the museum had more of those Reapers, it wasn't a bad option.

As long as the things still fired.

Sola continued. "Your real problem is going to be gathering any kind of fighting force worth a damn. The so-called militia has zero experience in firefights, as you've seen. Colonel Minh is full of good intentions, but he's more likely to drop a grenade at his feet than throw one."

Captain Zeno nodded in agreement. "The militia is raw, but with the right guidance, we can form them into a defensive unit for the city. Same goes for Minh. He's willing, I'll give him that. He'll follow orders."

He paused, considering, then looked over at Sam. "We'll need to gather what weapons we can, and put together a scouting mission. Thoughts, Sergeant?"

"Hall and Biel can handle weapons," Sam replied immediately. "I'd like to lead the scouting mission myself, sir."

He ignored Sola's raised eyebrow at this last remark.

"Good. Then this is what we're going to do: Sergeant Samson will take Bean, Troy, and Sola to scout the enemy and gather intel. Hall and Biel will assess the weapon stocks here. Moon, I want you to take a closer look into that chemical weapon and see if we can't turn it back on those cowards in some way. The rest of you are with me, preparing the local militia to defend the city. Oorah?"

"Oorah!" A chorus of voices sounded as everyone moved to obey their orders.

Bean and Troy trotted over to Sam and Sola.

"I assume Fenra's coming with us?" Sam asked Sola. "Because if so, she's going to need to take a bath. Doesn't matter how stealthy she is if the enemies smell her coming a mile away."

"Yeah, I'll let you tell her that," Sola said with a smirk.

Sam shook his head. "Fine. So what's the plan?"

Sola put a hand to her chest and adopted a look of innocence. "What, are you asking little old me? Didn't I hear that *you* were leading the scouting mission?"

Sam rolled his eyes. "Please. Let's not fight in front of the children." He tilted his head toward Bean and Troy, who both chuckled.

She grinned. "Okay. I know where the base is, or at least where it was not long ago. It wasn't much more than a campground the last time I saw it, so they could have moved easily enough, but I doubt it. It's not far, and I have transportation to get us there fast, but we should leave now. We'll want to use the cover of night, and I hope you all can swim."

"Swim?"

Sola winked. "You'll see."

CHAPTER 14

"I was going to bring my N-4, but with no ammo... well, it doesn't make a great club," Bean said to Sam as the legionnaires waited for Sola and Fenra at the front of the palace. "I wish we had something beyond knives and sidearms, though. I feel naked without a rifle."

"Interesting choice of words," Troy said, stroking his chin. "Maybe you're just insecure and that's why you *feel* naked."

"Maybe your mom is insecure," Bean said with a grin.

"Now why do you have to go and say a thing like that, Private Rivera?" Troy gave his friend's shoulder a good-natured punch. "Always got to go there. I'm beginning to think you have mommy issues."

"You're about to have busted lip issues in a second." Bean tried to keep a straight face but ended up cracking a grin.

Sam shook his head at the banter. "We'll see if we can get something from Sola before we leave."

Both his men gave him wide-eyed stares, and Troy waggled his eyebrows suggestively.

"Oh, no. It's not like that," Sam said, flustered. "She's—I'm sure she'll know where we can find reliable weapons."

Troy raised his hands and took a step back in surrender. "I didn't say anything, Sarge."

"Permission to speak freely, sir?" said Bean.

Sam didn't trust the mischievous twinkle in the man's eyes. "No, definitely not. Not on this subject. You two are like teenagers."

"I'm just saying, the heart wants what the heart wants..." Bean said under his breath.

She's just a guide and great in a fight, Sam thought. *Yeah, she's attractive. Nothing wrong with noticing that. But you have a job to do.*

Sola chose that awkward moment to appear. She jogged through the palace gate to join the legionnaires, a slight limp from her earlier injury still apparent. "You boys ready to rock and roll?" she said. "Fenra has the engine running."

"We're ready," Sam said, "except for weapons. All we have are our service pistols and knives."

"I'm way ahead of you," Sola said. "I have some weapons waiting for you on the *Hawk*, but we're killing daylight, so let's hustle." She took off at a jog.

"You have a ship?" Troy called as the leejes chased after her.

"Yep," Sola shouted back. "You'll see in a second."

The sky above Cononga was darkening, the sun having just dropped below the horizon, but it seemed as though most of the citizens of Noi were out and about, cleaning up bloodstains, repairing damage from the firefight, or just making the most of the cards life had dealt them.

A few stopped to wave at the legionnaires as they jogged past—and in their eyes Sam saw... respect. And hope.

He didn't get it earlier, but now he understood where that look came from. He knew what the Iron Wolves meant to these people. To their past... and now their future as well.

You're doing the right thing staying here, he told himself. *Come what may, you're doing the right thing.*

The run was much longer than Sola had suggested, but thanks to their Legion conditioning, the men had no trouble keeping pace. The guide led them out of town, away from the airfield, and weaved a trail through lush jungle foliage. She finally stopped beside a dark and muddy river that fed acres of rice paddies. Reeds poked up through the water like defensive quills.

Moored to a wooden pole and bobbing lazily amid the reeds was a small boat, about ten meters from stem to stern. And frankly, to call it a boat was being generous. It was better described as a piece of junk. Whatever paint it might once have had was a distant memory, and it was rusted so thoroughly that it looked like the whole thing could fall apart at any minute.

Fenra's lamp-like yellow eyes greeted them from out of the darkness. She stood on the boat's deck and howled what sounded like a welcome.

"Yes," Sola answered, looking over to Sam as she waded into the river. "The brave one came again. Don't embarrass yourself. After all, he's only alive because *you* saved him."

Sam followed Sola into the water and peered up at Fenra. The beast looked down at him with what could have been a toothy smile. Or an angry baring of her teeth. Sam hoped it was the former.

"Be careful here," Sola warned. "The rocks on the riverbed are very slippery. Your legionnaire armor won't help you with that."

"Actually, we got anti-slip soles, ma'am," said Bean.

Sam hid his grin as he followed Sola's path, trying to step where she stepped, but it was difficult to see in the darkness without his helmet. He'd kept it off during their run through the city, wanting to achieve a personal bond with those who saw him, but now he placed it on his head to take advantage of its low-light capabilities. It would be nice to know if there were any nasties swimming nearby, looking for a leej to chow.

Troy and Bean followed along behind.

"These rocks ain't so slippery," said Bean.

"And we're leejes." Troy thumped his chest and called after Sola. "Lady, I've charged entire Goliath battalions, tested my mettle against the best the Arch-Dread Army had to offer, and flown missions over the moons of Anak. Now watch as I conquer the legendary Slippery Rocks of Vi—"

His next words were lost in a splash as he disappeared under the water's murky surface.

Bean burst into laughter.

"Idiot," Sola muttered. She reached the boat, and a waiting Fenra hauled her inside. "You other legionnaires better hurry and get him up. His splashing will have alerted the monk eels."

"The monk who now?" Bean asked as a sputtering Troy regained his footing.

"Hurry up, you two," Sam said. He reached the boat right behind Sola. The lyconlore lifted him dangling into the air by his right arm, like a curious child lifting a dornbug off the ground.

Sam's feet hit the creaking deck of the rust bucket. As the shaggy lyconlore growled something that seemed friendly enough, then turned to help the other two legionnaires on board, Sam rubbed his shoulder. For a second there, he'd thought it might pop right out of the socket.

"The monk eels are predatory hunters that come out at night," Sola explained. "They're big. And very aggressive." She stepped into a cabin in the middle of the ship, barely large enough to house a single person plus the wheel.

At first Sam thought Sola was teasing. But the ripples that suddenly appeared in the water just past the stern made him think again. Something made a splash, but it was back below the surface too quickly for Sam to spot it.

"Hurry and get me out of here!" Troy pleaded with Fenra as the lyconlore lifted Bean onto the ship first. "I'm not built to fight water monsters. My skill set doesn't include that."

Fenra lifted Troy onto the boat, and Sola gunned the motor to life. It started with a heavy cough and a worrisome sputter, but settled into a dull hum.

From on board, the craft was even less impressive, which was really saying something. There were countless weld jobs keeping the thing whole, using a mishmash of metals from who knew what. The hull ended up looking like a patchwork quilt. Blaster fire had left dozens of scorch marks, and there were plenty of unpatched holes—fortunately above the waterline.

"No offense, Sola," Sam said, "but I've seen corpses that look healthier than this boat."

She gave a wry half smile. "You'd rather swim?"

"Not really. I mean, I'm grateful for the ride, but is this thing going to get us to the rebels and out? Emphasis on the 'out.' Like... what if we need to make a hasty retreat?"

Sola had the boat turned around and moved into the open river. "Don't you worry about the *Hawk*. She's never let me down before, and she doesn't plan to now." She increased their speed until they were skimming over the water.

Sam had to hold on to the railing to not lose his balance. Okay, so the boat was fast. He'd just have to pray that it waited to sink to the bottom of the river until *after* he'd safely stepped off.

"You need me to help guide you through the darkness?" he said, tapping his helmet. "Night vision."

Sola pointed to the sky overhead. "The stars are all I need to navigate. And if things get dicey, Fenra can see in the dark too. Take a load off, Sergeant. This isn't my first Balder hunt."

"Stars don't tell you when a log is sticking up in the mud," Sam muttered to himself, but he attempted what he thought would count as a relaxed position, leaning against the helmsman's cabin. "So..." he said. "How did you get involved in all this?"

"All what?" Sola asked.

Sam turned when he heard Fenra growling from across the deck. But she was merely "talking" with Troy and Bean, who were apparently doing their best to communicate with her through pantomime. The best Sam could tell, they were trying to say they were hungry. Sam shook his head at the sight and turned back to Sola.

"I guess what I'm saying is, how did you get to be the official guide for the Iron Wolves?" Sam realized that he was staring at her, taking her in with the aid of his night vision. This seemed somehow unfair. He took his bucket off, allowing the cool air to play with his hair. "You don't strike me as a part of the militia."

"You don't think I'm the sort who would help out of my own good nature?"

"No offense, but…"

Sola looked away from the helm with a playful smile on her full lips. "You know, just because you say 'no offense' doesn't give you the okay to say whatever you want *after* that."

"I didn't say *anything* after that," Sam said. "I just implied it." He crossed his arms over his chest. "But I'd still like to know the answer to the question."

Sola shrugged. "The president wanted the best guide money could buy. Fenra and I have a reputation for getting things done. When we heard the price he was offering, we came."

"Yeah… I'm not buying it."

"Excuse me?"

"You heard me. No way you took this job for the money."

"Oh, really?"

"Yes, really, because you're here, and this isn't the type of thing people who want money do. No sense in taking a risk like this if you're ever looking to actually spend that money. So spill it."

Sola studied Sam with a raised eyebrow. "Perhaps my ancestors also fought alongside the Iron Wolves during the Savage Wars. Maybe I grew up on stories myself and wanted to see with my own eyes if they were true or not."

That was something Sam could almost believe. "And?"

"And what?"

"Are the stories true?"

"Too soon to tell." Sola cocked her head to one side, letting the wind blow her hair over her shoulder. "You know, when this is all over... I mean, I don't know what legionnaire protocol is on..."

BOOM!

The ship shook with such sudden violence that Sam was sent sprawling across the deck. A moment later he was up, helmet on, and looking to confirm that Troy and Bean were still topside and not in the water. "What was that?"

"Monk eels," Sola said through gritted teeth. "Fenra! Get the weapons and then take the wheel!"

CHAPTER 15

Fenra tore into a long steel box on the starboard side of the ship, flinging metal couplings across the deck, and retrieved three long spears in her massive paw. She handed each legionnaire a spear as though she were running an armory, then sprinted for Sola's place at the helm.

"What the heck is this?" Bean said, looking at his spear. "This isn't a weapon! It's a stick with a piece of metal on the end. What am I supposed to do with this?"

"I think she wants us to throw it?" Troy speculated.

The *Hawk* shuddered from another impact beneath the waterline. The deck had grown slick with the spray of the river, and Sam found himself tumbling over the knee-high railing at the side. He grabbed on to a baluster at the last moment, a lucky grope in the dark that seemed a miracle.

"Help!" he shouted, feeling his boots skipping along the surface of the river, the drag threatening to break his grip on the wet metal.

Through his HUD, he saw the boat's wake thrashing as if it had come alive. Then a serpentine head rose above the surface—just for a split second, but long enough for Sam to take in the primal terror of the monk eel. Its luminescent green eyes shone with predatory intent, and its elongated snout, filled with razor-sharp teeth, snapped.

Judging by the size of the head alone, the entire eel had to be at least as long as the *Hawk.*

"Pull me up! Now!" Sam shouted.

Troy appeared at the railing and thrust out an arm. "I got you, Sarge!"

Bean appeared beside him, and the two leejes pulled Sam back on board with a heave.

"Thanks, guys," Sam said, lying on the deck. "Holy sket, Sola, we need to talk about your definition of an eel. That's not an eel. That's the thing that ate all the other eels and absorbed their power. It's the eel *god.*"

Sola didn't reply. She was standing perfectly still on the stern of the speeding boat, her knees absorbing the up-and-down bob of the waves. She held a spear in her right hand, arm cocked back and poised to throw.

A flurry of motion sent the water spraying upward as a dark-skinned eel erupted from the river's surface, lunging for Sola with its greedy mouth open, its sharp triangles of teeth gleaming in the moonlight.

But the spear was hurtling through the air before the creature's head even fully cleared the water. Its pointed tip entered the monk eel through its open mouth and continued right on through the back of its head.

The eel didn't go down immediately. It jerked its head around, the shaft of the spear still lodged in its mouth, battering the boat with resounding clangs, before sinking beneath the water.

"Don't just stand there!" Sola shouted as she grabbed another spear. "More will be coming!"

"How many of them are there?" Sam asked. He positioned himself beside Sola, while Troy and Bean took port and starboard watch. "And why aren't we using *actual* weapons, like blasters?"

Given how ably Sola had dispatched the first eel, clearly the spears *were* actual weapons—in the right hands, but Sam's finger was made for a trigger, not a pointy stick.

"They hunt in packs," Sola answered, not taking her eyes from the water. "Figure at least three... but maybe ten. It's not a coincidence you don't see any other ships out here. There's a reason no one travels at night."

"You know," said Bean, "this is exactly the kind of thing I dreamed of when I joined the Legion. Riding on a rusted boat down an alien river, heading to a rebel base, with nothing but sticks for weapons, and being attacked by sea monsters."

"Correction." Troy looked over at his buddy with a grin. "*River* monsters. And I still got a tiny bit of charge left in my blaster pistol."

"No! Blasters will only draw more attention!" Sola eyed the water next to where Sam stood. She pointed an outstretched finger. "There!"

Sam saw it. Just below the dark surface of the water, two glowing green orbs raced toward him.

Grasping his spear with both hands, he plunged it into the dark head of the eel. The steel point sliced into the creature's soft skin like a sharp knife through a piece of raw meat. The eel broke off its attack run, and Sam was just able to yank his spear out of the eel's body before it disappeared again.

"We are not your dinner!" Troy shouted as he drove his spear into another charging eel. "Just leave us alone!"

Despite the insanity of the situation he found himself in—or perhaps because of it—Sam cracked a wide grin inside his helmet. Sometimes when plans went to hell, you *had* to laugh about them. Surrender to the absurdity.

They had to withstand two more attack runs before the massive eels decided that legionnaires came at too high of a cost to be included on their menu. Still, they stood vigilant for several minutes longer before Sola called out, "I think they've gone."

"How can you be sure?" Sam asked.

"I can't, but we need rest." Sola lowered her spear and returned it to the long metal box Fenra had taken it from. "If they come back we'll do it all over again, but there's no sense in tiring ourselves out before then. You legionnaires get some sleep. Fenra and I will take turns navigating the waters and keeping watch."

Sam removed his helmet again. "You sure I can't help?"

"There's no point. You don't know the river. Grab some sleep while you can. You're going to need it when we get to the rebel encampment."

Sam didn't argue—because she was right. He plopped down in the back of the boat with the other two legionnaires, intending to at least feign sleep—if he could—long enough to be sure he was with friends.

"I could drive the boat. It can't be too different from piloting a ship," Troy said removing his helmet.

"No, she'll be fine," Sam said as he tried to find the least uncomfortable position for sleeping. "Our turn is tomorrow. Sleep. We've got a long day ahead."

"We've got a long night ahead with the way Troy talks in his sleep," Bean said. "Full-on reciting dark poetry while he's knocked out."

"That was one time, and it wasn't poetry," Troy said, lying on his side between Sam and Bean. "They were tough-guy quotes."

"Yeah sure, whatever you say. You were the one sleeping, so of course you'd know."

Sam gazed up into the night sky. Cononga's twin moons were high overhead, and the stars twinkled on and off like tiny lights someone had stuck into a dark ceiling. On planets like this, the night sky often appeared to be made more of stars than of empty space.

Sleep came quickly. Sam was exhausted, and his body needed time to rest and repair, but as on so many other nights, with sleep came nightmares.

CHAPTER 16

This particular nightmare was a familiar one. Different variations of it had plagued Sam since his early years as a legionnaire. It always started the same.

"Incoming enemy fire!"

Someone always shouted that. Every time.

Next would come the mortars, grenades, and blaster rounds.

Sam was entrenched in a foxhole with a platoon of legionnaires. Faces he recognized looked back at him, bracing for the first rounds of fire. These men were about to die. They didn't know it yet. Sam did.

He'd been there.

But in the dream, the men were still alive. They hunkered down low to his left and his right, their breathing heavy.

Breathing.

They wouldn't live.

They never did.

BOOM! BOOM! BOOM!

The first rounds of artillery came in with a furious intensity. It was like being caught in a sudden, violent thunderstorm, flashes of lightning overpowering the night. The explosions threatened to burst his eardrums despite his helmet—that was the dream weaving its fiction—and the flashes did their best to eviscerate corneas.

Sam's heart beat in his chest as fast as he could ever remember it. Adrenaline's icy flow raced to flood every inch of his being.

"Pour it on 'em, boys! Let 'em have it!"

The voice belonged to a hardscrabble first sergeant named Jeff Howard. This was a detail the dream got wrong. The *real* Howard didn't shout that until the artillery had stopped and the advance had started.

In the nightmare, it all happened at once. The shelling and the fighting.

The living and the dying.

"Oorah!" the legionnaires responded.

A leej on Sam's left raised his head above the foxhole and leveled his N-4 at the charging enemy. "Get some!"

This time they were being attacked by zhee. In other versions of the nightmare, it was other species. That part of the nightmare changed.

The worst version was the one where the attackers were the dead legionnaires. Sam's old friends. In that version, he was alone in that foxhole.

Every legionnaire fighting with Sam would die. *Had* died. He'd seen it. Not all at once, like the nightmarish final battle suggested, but he'd seen it. Guys got unlucky on some rotation out to the edge. A speeder or shuttle wreck here. A sniper there. An IED. There were a million ways to die, and Sam knew the faces of those deaths. Of the men beneath the buckets. Those faces cycled in his mind. Dead soldiers. Dead friends.

Brothers he could never forget.

"Get your weapon up, Samson!" First Sergeant Howard bellowed. "We got a target-rich environment here, boy!"

Sam looked over the ridge of dirt. The zhee were gone. Replacing them was a line of politicians, advancing in white suits with gleaming shoes. They carried blasters, and they smirked and grinned each time a blaster bolt fired by a legionnaire struck them harmlessly.

"Bring it!" First Sergeant Howard cried, standing up to unleash a volley of fire.

"No!" Sam screamed, fumbling to grab his first sergeant and drag him down behind cover.

But it was too late. Because in the dream, it was always too late.

A spray of blood and gore washed over him. The first sergeant's head, which only moments before had been swearing vengeance and wrath, was now a hollow crater of charred meat and chipped bone. Howard's body fell hard into the foxhole, spasming as though it were trying to somehow rise up headless.

"We gotta get out of here, man!" The legionnaire on Sam's left grabbed at his arm in a panic. "We gotta go! We gotta—"

A mortar exploded at the leej's feet, throwing bits of him all over Sam.

Sam knew the mortar should have killed him too, but he didn't die. He lived. In the dream, he only stood there, wiping the blood off of his visor.

His ears rang. His body felt like pins and needles.

He looked down at the corpse at his feet. The guy's bucket had been blown off his head, and Sam could see his face plainly. He was still a kid. Just a kid. Though when the real kid had died, he and Sam were the same age and rank.

They were friends.

That ghostly face looked up at him now. Forever static at twenty years old.

"Help me up," the dead legionnaire said.

Sam lifted the man up and cradled him in his arms. The back side of the leej was basically gone, shredded from his body, like a butcher taking meat away from bone.

Blood spilled from the kid's lips and eyes as he looked up at Sam. "I just want to go home," he begged, as if Sam could somehow make that happen. "I just want to see... see my mom again."

Sam hushed the legionnaire. Rocked him back and forth. Ignored all the hell that was breaking loose around them. The battle—the war—didn't matter. All he could think about was the kid in his arms.

"Shhh. You'll see her soon, buddy. I promise."

When the dead legionnaire—PFC Allen Valdes—had really died, in the aftermath of an assault shuttle crash just outside Camp Trigget on Grevulo, Sam saw it happen. He was patrolling the camp's perimeter, and his squad was the first to the crash site. The bird was part of a QRF looking to pull out some marines who'd gotten into trouble. The flight lasted all of thirty seconds before it went down hard.

Sam watched PFC Valdes die. Not in the dream. In real life. Sam heard the kid ask the squad's medic about his mom, just like in the dream, and right before Valdes passed, he seemed at peace.

"I'll see her soon," he said, and then he was gone.

But in the dream, he didn't say that. He always said:

"Why? Why all of this? What is it for?"

"Easy now," Sam replied. Tears fell down his hardened face, unaccompanied by sobs. Just a stoic, familiar hot sting in his eyes. "Rest, brother. It's okay. I've got you."

"Make this count." The kid's eyes went wide as the last gasp of oxygen escaped his lungs. "Make this all count for something. Promise me."

The Legion once made Sam talk with a medical bot programmed with all the latest psychoanalysis software. The bot told Sam that this part of the dream was representative of his desire to bring meaning to the death of every legionnaire. An impossibility, the bot said.

Sam didn't mention the version of the dream where the members of the House of Reason were the enemy combatants. He knew enough to keep that much quiet.

"I will," Sam said to the kid.

To Allen.

Then the kid died in his arms, his head lolling sideways like a stage actor performing his big death scene.

A manic insanity seized Sam at that moment. He rocked back and forth, hugging the kid tightly despite the chaos around them.

"I promise!" he roared over the sounds of war. "I'll make this count. I'll find a way!"

"Sam!"

The voice seemed to be calling to him from the other side.

"Sam!"

He snapped out of the nightmare to find Sola kneeling beside him. Her eyes, usually narrow with scorn and rebellion, were now wide with concern. The moons and stars overhead gave her an ethereal glow that played against her white hair.

"I'm good," Sam said, propping himself up. Sounding better than he felt. A cold sweat drenched his brow, and as he moved, it ran down to his neckline. "Yeah, I'm... I'm fine."

"You were screaming in your sleep." Sola spoke softly. "You're very clearly *not* okay. I'm surprised you didn't wake up those two."

Sam looked to his right. Troy and Bean lay sound asleep. Troy was murmuring something that sounded like poetry. "Yea, though I walk through..."

Sam knew the line. Troy was fond of delivering it. "Yea, though I walk through the valley of the shadow of death, I will fear no evil. For I am the evilest one in this valley."

Evidently he liked it so much that he repeated it in his sleep.

Sola took a seat next to Sam. Her gaze was far off, as if she were looking into the past itself. "There's no shame in memories that haunt us," she said. "We all have them to one extent or another."

The way she said it made Sam feel like she knew what she was talking about. Like she, too, was forced to remember events she would rather have buried.

"I guess it comes with the job." Sam cleared his throat. "How long have I been asleep?"

Sola ignored the question. Apparently she wasn't going to let him change the subject. "Talking about your dreams is the best way to deal with them. It's hard at first. But... it doesn't really get any easier without it. You'll get stronger. You'll learn to live with it."

"I don't want to talk about it," Sam said. He heard the edge in his voice, and was surprised at how strongly he felt about this, but that wasn't the only reason he resisted. His pride resented Sola telling him how it was. He was a legionnaire. No one knew how it was as well as he did.

Then again, no one had ever really pushed him to talk about his nightmares, either. Except for the one time. When the point—who was in all honesty probably trying to be helpful—ordered him to speak to that bot.

Sam sighed. "I'm sorry. I know you're just trying to help."

"I understand."

"Thanks. Can we drop this until another time?" Sam knew that such a time would likely never occur. Cononga was her planet, not his. He'd be out as soon as the mission was completed. Maybe sooner.

"Sure." Sola stood up and dusted off her hands. "You should probably wake up your friends. The sun will be up before we know it. We've made good time toward the rebel camp."

"It's been that long? I feel like I just closed my eyes."

"You slept for a few hours. Not nearly what your body needs."

"Story of my life," Sam said, stretching his back and legs.

He looked overboard and watched the water fly by. The ship's deck stabilizers kept things from getting too bumpy—at least that much of the old boat hadn't rusted out.

"You weren't kidding when you said this ship of yours could move."

"She's been through a lot, but she's still a beast," Sola said, she poked her head into the boat's cabin, which was currently manned by Fenra. The lyconlore's huge bulk in the small helm area looked almost comical. Sola fumbled for something outside of Sam's view and came up with a canteen and a few bars in white wrappers. "Here. Breakfast is served."

"What is this?" Sam said, catching one of the bars in midair. "Or do I even want to know?"

"I wouldn't want to know if I were you." Sola winked. "But I'll tell you if you want."

Fenra caught Sam's eye and shook her head furiously in warning.

"I... think I'll pass on hearing the ingredient list," Sam said.

"Smart boy. Then let's just say it's everything your body needs to keep going." Sola took a huge bite of her bar, chewed it a few times, and pushed it into a large wad on the side of her mouth. "Minus the taste."

She tossed him two more bars for Bean and Troy. He dropped the food onto their chests, waking them up.

"Breakfast in bed, Sarge?" Bean sat up blinking. "Aw. You shouldn't have."

Troy rubbed the sleep from his eyes. "Oh, guys, I had the *craziest* dream. We were attacked by giant eels, and a huge lyconlore was piloting us on a rust bucket of a boat, and—" Troy's stopped short upon seeing Sola's glare. "Okay." He shrugged. "Not funny. I get it."

"Dude, you're *never* funny," Bean said. "I keep telling you you're not a comedian."

Troy sighed. "Guess the dream of serving as a leej continues."

"Eat up," Sam said. Not for the first time around these two, he felt like a stern father corralling his goofball teenage sons. "We'll be at the rebel encampment soon."

"I'll eat it, but... what *is* it?" Troy asked. He took a bite.

"Apparently it's better not to know," Sam replied.

He bit into his own bar. It was chalky and tasted... healthy. Whatever that meant. Like a chewy, chalky mass of mush you might buy for too many credits at the gym as a post-workout meal. His jaw was getting some exercise, too, but the thing softened the more Sam chewed. He'd eaten worse. Much worse.

"You know what this tastes like?" Troy said. "Like that one time we found that hot meal still on the grill after we caught those Zarlings by surprise."

Sam grunted in agreement.

The first glow of the sun crested over the horizon. Fenra reduced throttle and the wind died down. In its absence, a sticky, early morning humidity fogged the deck.

"We should be quiet from here on out," Sola said, eyeing the river's still waters. Dense foliage crowded the banks on either shore. "We're close."

CHAPTER 17

The river narrowed to ten feet on either side of the boat. Roots and tree limbs hung over the banks as though the jungle were attempting to swallow up the waterway.

Sam chased the last of his breakfast with a long swig of cold canteen water. He placed his bucket back on his head and linked up with the captain.

"Captain Zeno, this is Sergeant Samson. Come in."

"I have a copy, Samson," Captain Zeno replied a moment later.

"Guide says we're close to the rebel encampment. I'll contact you again when we're on our way back."

The boat glided quietly to a halt next to an outcropping of dense brush. Hopefully that would be enough to hide the craft from anyone who didn't float in the way they'd come.

"Understood," Captain Zeno said. "Remember, your mission is not to engage. Assess the threat and return back to base."

"Roger that, sir."

"Sergeant. I know you. Do *not* engage."

"Yes, sir."

The comm inside his helmet clicked, signaling the transmission had come to an end.

Sola beckoned the three legionnaires over to her, then pulled out a heavy-looking chest from near the bow. "Weapons. Pick what you'd like."

"Oooh, I hope it's more spears," Bean quipped.

"Pickings are slim," Sola said, popping the lid with the toe of her boot. "But you're welcome to whatever you like."

Sam looked down at an assortment of weapons: knives and machetes, hand blasters and rifles, grenades and charge packs.

"You'll probably only be interested in—" Sola's stopped as the legionnaires dug into the pile of weapons like a group of hungry kids at a buffet. "Never mind. Just take everything, why don't you? That works too."

Sam lifted a long-barreled blaster that looked like it had seen better years. The last time it was fired in anger was probably sometime in the Savage Wars, but the charge pack was full, and a spare was banded around the weapon's stock. This one was a keeper. Next he picked up a snub-nosed blaster pistol, fat and heavy. Probably good for one, maybe two shots. But better than nothing.

Troy found a ranged heavy blaster that looked like it could fit on the turret of a tank. "What is this thing?"

Bean dug deep and pulled out a long belt of bullets. "Think these go with it. Slug thrower."

Troy fed the belt into the machine gun and draped it over his neck. It hung down to his knees. There might once have been some kind of case meant to store the bullets more efficiently, but it had probably disappeared long ago.

"Cool," Troy said. "I'm gonna take some of these frag-gers, too."

Bean chose a blaster that looked similar to Sola's Reaper 210, then held up a machete that wasn't too rusted and gave it an appraising frown. Finally he plucked out two grenades and hung them on his belt. "Oughta be enough to KTF, right, Sarge?"

"No KTF today," Sam answered. "Captain's orders."

"Like I could if I wanted to," Troy said, struggling with the dangling belt of ammunition. "Help me with this, Bean?"

Bean scoffed but relented. He draped the belt around his own shoulders. "What are friends for?"

"You two going to walk side by side through the jungle like that?" Sola said. "A couple of lovers holding hands on a stroll?"

"Oh, I know she did not just go there," said Troy.

Sam put a hasty end to the banter. "She's got a point. That thing looks like it can spit out some serious fire if it comes down to it, but we're on recon. We can't have that ammo belt jingling around through the jungle."

"I think I can find a satchel to store it in," Sola said.

Sam couldn't help but notice something was bothering her. "Everything all right?" he asked.

"Just... be careful with those weapons. It took me more than a few years to stockpile this little armory."

"Ma'am," Bean said, giving a slight bow, "no one takes better care of weapons than a legionnaire."

"That's right," Troy agreed. "We take care of 'em 'cause they take care of us. *Oorah*." The legionnaire looked down into the chest. "Hey. What's this?"

As he bent down to remove a long file, Bean had to struggle to keep the ammo belt from falling off. Troy made a stabbing motion with the file. "This for guttin' the enemy or something?"

"Looks like a prison shank," Bean said.

Fenra finished mooring the boat and came over to the others. She plucked the item from Troy's hand and began filing her long nails into fine, dagger-like points.

"That's Fenra's grooming tool," Sola said. "But she'll use it as a shank if you try to keep it from her."

Troy looked up at the big lyconlore. "Nah. That's all yours, big girl."

Sola hopped over the side of the boat and splashed into waist-high water. "Let's go. We have a hike to the rebel camp."

Sam followed Sola's lead, but managed to land in water that was chest-deep. He waded to the shore. "Bean, take point."

"Yes, sir." The legionnaire hustled over the side and sloshed ahead in front of Sola.

"He doesn't even know where we're going," Sola protested.

"You can tell him," said Sam, almost overtaking her. "But what you can't do is use all the sensors he has inside his bucket."

As the guide, the lyconlore, and the three legionnaires traversed the dense jungle of Cononga, everything was foreign to Sam. The foliage of bright greens, purples, and browns. The otherworldly howls of unseen animals. The chirps, clicks, and caws.

The one thing that was decidedly not foreign to Sam was the threat of armed hostiles on the other side of every branch, rock, and tree.

Sweat beaded on his forehead as the sun lifted into the sky. His bucket and suit had climate controls, but they could only do so much during a long, hard march.

After a time, Fenra sniffed the air, then broke off from the main group, hardly making a sound as she disappeared into the jungle.

"Where's she off to?" Sam whispered.

"Scouting," Sola answered.

A bright red-and-blue bird flew overhead, and the heavy flapping of its wings caused all four of them to raise their weapons skyward. In a tree high above them, some sort of chubby, bear-like simian with four red eyes gave a howl that sounded a lot like a laugh. From somewhere off to the party's left, a hissing creature scurried through the underbrush.

Sam didn't mind the sounds of alien wildlife. It was when the critters ceased making their natural sounds that he had to worry.

Another hour passed before Sam finally asked the question that he himself always hated being asked while on patrol. "How much farther?"

Sola was just in front of him, behind Troy, who was pulling a turn on point. She wiped a slender arm across her brow. "Not much. We should—"

A crashing through the brush stilled her words. Everyone in the patrol crouched and pointed their weapons to the source of the noise. Whatever it was, it sounded big—possibly multiple bigs.

Sam's heart raced as he thought of just how old his weapon probably was. He was going to be pissed if the weapon didn't fire.

Just squeeze the trigger. What happens after that is beyond your control.

The rustling noise increased, and Fenra emerged from the foliage.

Sola lowered her blaster. "What the heck?"

Sam was surprised himself. The shaggy lyconlore had certainly left quietly. Perhaps she'd deliberately made a lot of noise on the way back to avoid startling the patrol.

"We were about to kill you," Sola said. "What happened to the sign we agreed on?"

Fenra looked confused. Her yellow eyes widened as she growled something.

"'What sign'?" Sola put her hands on her hips. "What do you mean, 'what sign'? Did you honestly forget? How many concussions *have* you had? We agreed on the low bark." Sola acted as though she were clapping her hands, but stopped short before skin could smack skin. "Two barks. Pause. Then one more. Remember?"

Fenra crossed her arms and said something else in her guttural tongue.

"Fenra. I didn't mean it like—"

Fenra growled again.

"For Oba's sake, I know you're not a dog. When I said 'bark,' I—"

Again Fenra stubbornly growled.

"Fine. We're going to talk about this another time," Sola said, sounding exasperated.

Troy and Bean snickered to each other over L-comm.

"Did you find anything?" Sola asked.

Fenra made motions with her paws and spoke more of her language. Sam had hoped his bucket's AI might be able to make some sense of it, but lyconlores had extremely varied dialects, and Fenra's apparently wasn't in the databanks.

"What's she saying?" he asked.

"That the rebels aren't far from here," Sola said. "She'll take us in if you can bear not to have one of your leejes on point."

Sam nodded. "Okay. Let's do it."

Sola nodded back. "Just step where we step."

"It's not our first time around the junkyard," Sam replied as Sola and Fenra took the lead. "No offense."

"None taken," Sola said.

They moved quickly and quietly. Sola seemed impressed that the legionnaires were able to keep up. "How you boys move quietly in those armored suits is beyond me," she whispered.

"You'd be surprised what you can get used to."

As the small force crept forward, silence fell around them, and not only due to a lack of conversation—this silence came from the jungle itself. The animals of the jungle were giving the rebel base a healthy buffer.

It wasn't long before Sam's bucket picked up the distant sound of heavy vehicles and men's voices. He held up a fist to stop Bean and Troy, then motioned for them to hug the dirt. Sola and Fenra likewise got down on their bellies, and the party slid through the jungle like exotic snakes.

Sam held his weapon across his arms, in the crooks of his elbows. The going was slow and painful, but finally they stopped behind a fallen tree covered by an overhang of vines from another tree. It was a perfect vantage point from which to spy on what lay ahead.

Wedged between Sola and Fenra, with Troy and Bean watching their flanks and rear, Sam activated his bucket's zoom options.

They were atop a hill that fell away steeply into a wide valley teeming with rebels. The valley had been cleared of vegetation to make room for the base, which was way larger than Sam was expecting.

He scanned the compound, taking in as much as he could.

What he saw made his mouth go dry.

CHAPTER 18

The compound was square, with guard towers in each corner. Sentries guarded the perimeter, and more sentries were stationed by what Sam figured to be the barracks, armory, and mess hall. The rebel guards wore black vests—they looked to be some kind of body armor—and each was equipped with an open-faced helmet similar to those of the Republic marines. Just inside the gate, trucks were loaded down with supplies and probably weapons. One flatbed had its massive contents covered with a dark green tarp.

But what concerned Sam the most was the sheer size of the rebel operation. He'd expected an encampment of... dozens, maybe. This was a full-fledged base, with hundreds of troops moving around, and they were making obvious preparations to leave. Sam could make an educated guess as to where they were going.

"There's so many of them," Troy breathed, barely audible. "What do you think, Sarge? Three hundred?"

"More." Sam was working on a count of men, weapons, and equipment for Captain Zeno. "Four hundred at least.

Most are unarmored, but I bet they'll repurpose those transport vehicles before the fighting starts."

"If they leave today and travel hard," Sola whispered, "they'll reach Noi in two days."

"We need to get closer to find out exactly what we're up against," Sam said. He hated to endanger his men, but accurate intel could mean the difference between life and death in the coming days. "In particular, I'd like to know what's under the tarp on that flatbed. Sola, Fenra, circle to the right. Gather whatever intel you can, but stay covered. We'll do the same from the left."

"Got it," Sola said.

Sam was surprised she didn't zing him with some sharp retort. Maybe the two of them were simply on the same wavelength. "Meet back here in thirty minutes."

"You think they've got some kind of weapon on that truck?" Bean whispered.

"That's my guess," Sam said, crouch-walking through the jungle. "If we can find out, maybe we can be prepared to neutralize it when the fighting starts."

"Or," Troy said with a heavy breath, "and just hear me out here, Sarge—we could destroy it now and make sure it never gets into the city at all."

"I'd like nothing more," Sam said. He'd already thought of the possibility. "But Captain Zeno wants us on this scouting mission as eyes only."

The trio of legionnaires had just fallen to their stomachs to crawl forward when an eruption of blaster fire came from the opposite side of the camp.

"Sket!" Sam hissed. He elbow-crawled through foliage until he had a clear view of the base. Shouting voices drifted up to him, but the rebels weren't keyed in on his location. They were racing the opposite way.

Sam's stomach twisted as he saw Sola being dragged out of the jungle by two men. She fought like a demon, twisting and turning to get out of her captors' grip.

"Easy, Sola," Sam muttered to himself.

"She's gonna get herself killed," said Bean, crawling up beside him.

Sola punched one of her captors in the groin. As the man let go of her arm, she rose to her knees and head-butted the other rebel. She regained her feet, but the first man tackled her to the ground almost immediately, and the two rebels began to beat her savagely.

Bean shared a look with Troy. "Sarge? Orders?"

How much is a life worth? Sam thought to himself. Attempting to save Sola's life would jeopardize not only Sam's, but those of his men as well.

But Sola had risked her life to save Sam and his men. Just the fact that she was out here with them was a risk. He owed her an attempt.

"We go and get her," Sam said, handing his weapon to Bean. "I want both of you to stay here to provide points of divergent cover fire. I didn't see Fenra, so watch your fire when things get fun, just in case they didn't already drop her out in the jungle. And if things get too hairy, both of you haul ass to the boat and get out of here."

"No way, Sarge," Bean protested. "We're—"

"I'm not *asking* you, Private Rivera," Sam growled with a tone Captain Zeno would have been proud of. "I'm *telling* you. The captain needs this intel. And he'll need every leej he can get for the defense of Noi. If I go down, you two get out of here and don't look back. Oorah?"

"Oorah," Bean and Troy said together. They sounded less than thrilled.

Sam unsheathed the blade from his belt and worked his way slowly down an uneven hill. He felt as though his senses were on overdrive as he attempted to take in the terrain around him as well as keep an eye on what was happening with Sola.

A hundred yards ahead were two rebels with their backs turned to Sam. They were obviously supposed to be guarding the perimeter, but they were clearly more interested in seeing what was taking place on the other side of the base.

In his mind's eye, Sam visualized what would come next.

Neutralize the two guards to get inside the perimeter. Move between the vehicles to stay covered. Wait for an opening to grab Sola, then run like the dogs of hell are at your heels.

Sam repeated the plan in his mind. It was as good as he could do under the circumstances. And it might even work.

Except something is going to go wrong. Something always goes wrong.

Sam shook his head fractionally. What would be would be. *Adapt. Adapt and survive.*

He was twenty yards from the two sentries when a rotten branch snapped beneath his foot. One of the rebels turned. His eyes widened upon seeing the legionnaire stalking him from the jungle, his mouth opened to shout a warning, and his rifle came up.

Already charging, seeking to close ground, Sam flung his blade forward. The knife drove itself up to the hilt into the sentry's throat. Blood spurted from the wound as the rebel choked and sank to his knees.

The other guard turned to watch his friend fall, his face registering shock before he wheeled around to face the legionnaire crashing full-speed through the undergrowth, but he turned too late.

Sam drove his elbow into the guard's nose, shattering it. He pulled the blade from the dying rebel's throat and slammed it up through the other guard's jaw, pinning his mouth shut. He slipped around behind the rebel, clamped his hand over his mouth, and snapped his neck with a vicious wrench.

The two deaths had been fast and brutal, but most importantly, they had been undetected.

Sam looked down at the corpses. In times like these he found himself detaching from reality. Drifting away from the things that he was ordering his body to do. He took no pleasure in death. He didn't relish the idea of sticking another living being like he had, but the decision to do just that had been a simple one. It was him or them.

He moved on, keeping low to the ground as he hastened for the armada of vehicles now between him and Sola.

He could hear her being jeered at. Mocked. It nauseated him. Female captives were rarely treated with respect.

He had to hurry.

He crouched down at the side of a small truck mounted with a heavy blaster cannon. It marked the farthest point he could reach without stepping out into the open.

"Am I good?" he asked over L-comm.

"Yeah, you're clear," answered Bean. "Sola... not so much."

As Sam crept to the edge of the truck, trying to get eyes on Sola, he heard a familiar voice from her direction.

"Well, well, well, what do we have here?"

Sam peered around the truck. Standing in front of Sola was the officer who'd worked him over back in that alley. The officer whose face Fenra had carved up with her wicked claws. His face was bandaged, but his sneering tone was unchanged.

"A Conongan scout sneaking around our perimeter?" he said, looking down at Sola. "A soldier maybe? You're not exactly... dressed for the part."

The rebels around him hooted and laughed.

The man stepped to one side, and Sam got his first good look at Sola. Her clothing was tattered and pulled away; many hands had already been at her before this officer came in to take control of the situation. Her face was mottled and red; soon, no doubt, bruises would begin to form, but she looked as defiant as ever.

Sam had an idea. An insane idea, but it might just get both him and Sola out of here.

And yet... only a few vehicles to the south, the massive truck with the green tarp draped over it sat begging to be investigated. Calling him away. Reminding him that the reason Sola was captured was because they agreed they needed to know what secrets lay under that covering.

"Troy. Bean. You still have eyes on me?"

"Yes, Sergeant."

"Good. Get down here and take up a firing position at my location. One of you get on this truck's mounted gun, the other support with small arms. And be ready to start the rig up."

"*That's* what I'm talking about," said Bean.

Sam appreciated the mettle of his legionnaires. "Open up on the rebels as soon as you get here. I'll grab Sola, and we'll use the vehicle to escape. Go now."

"Roger that," Troy said.

Sam didn't waste time watching to make sure his leejes reached his position. Not with things escalating with Sola and the green-skinned commander, and not while he needed to get a look underneath that tarp. He started toward the covered truck.

"I'm not a soldier," Sola shouted at the officer. "Or a mercenary bottom-feeder like you!"

Sam didn't think Sola was doing herself any favors, but her reply was more or less what he would have said in her situation.

"You know nothing about me, Conongan trash!" The commander slapped Sola and drew a curved blade from his belt. It looked more like a hook than a knife. "And you know nothing about the purpose I serve."

"Then enlighten me," Sola said spitting a mouthful of blood to the side. She was held down, on her knees, with a rebel soldier on either side holding back her arms. Talking was about all she was capable of doing. And breathing. Though neither of those capabilities seemed guaranteed for long. Not with the way things were going.

"I serve a greater purpose." The commander opened his arms, stretching them out to encompass the entirety of the base and the rebels within. "A purpose these men understand. The Republic's 'democracy' will weaken the nation of Cononga, and with it, the entire planet. People are too stupid to make decisions by themselves. They're a flock of foolish animals that need direction. No, the people of Cononga need to be united under one ruler."

"Sounds like slavery to me," Sola said, keeping her eyes on the commander.

As Sam reached the truck, he caught just a glimpse of something large and gray flashing in the jungle. Fenra was alive. That changed things.

He looked behind him. Troy and Bean were already setting up shop on the back of the vehicle.

Things were about to get crazy, and before that happened, he was going to see what was underneath that tarp.

He untied a cord from the tarp's eyelet and lifted the canvas up to peer inside. It was dark, and none of his bucket's vision modes—infrared, thermal, digital echolocation mapping—revealed the full picture, but they provided enough for him to piece things together.

It wasn't good.

CHAPTER 19

The largest cannon Sam had ever seen was in pieces in the back of the truck. He couldn't be sure of its strength without knowing its energy source, but any weapon of this size had to be powerful. The barrel alone was big enough for him to crawl inside.

He captured several images of the weapon with his bucket. Maybe Captain Zeno would have a better idea of what this thing was.

As he popped back out from beneath the tarp, he heard shouting.

"There's another one!" one of the rebels yelled.

Fenra's massive frame was too large not to be seen. The hulking lyconlore had apparently been rummaging through a supply truck when she was spotted. How she'd even gotten that far without being noticed was a mystery. Stealth could only do so much for you when you were an eight-foot-tall furry beast.

It didn't matter. The three legionnaires were about to have been spotted anyway. Troy and Bean had set up in the back of the technical truck, with Bean standing at the heavy blaster cannon in the truck-bed and Troy standing beside him, hefting his old belt-fed machine gun. The pair of legionnaires unleashed a scorching rate of fire that sent the base into immediate chaos. All around, rebel soldiers dove for cover or were torn to shreds.

It's now or never. Time to rock and roll.

Sam sprinted toward Sola. He didn't bother with cover now, running right among the rebels who were frantically seeking cover. Most seemed terrified at the appearance of another legionnaire; likely they believed that their base was under a coordinated Legion assault, but one drew a blaster pistol and attempted to line Sam up in his sights.

Sam was a ghost, darting in and sidestepping the weapon. He grabbed the rebel's wrist, twisting it until he heard a pop and saw the weapon drop to the ground. That was followed up by a helmeted head-butt that sent the rebel down in a heap.

Sam stooped to retrieve the blaster and continued toward Sola.

The element of surprise was still on their side, but Sam had been in enough fights to know that that advantage was quickly fading. In seconds, the rebels would determine where the fire was coming from and how many were in the opposition. Then they'd rally, and with the numbers advantage they enjoyed, the return fire would surely overwhelm the steady clip Troy and Bean were laying down.

Sam skidded to a halt before Sola. "Hey, thought you could use a hand," he said with a grin.

She clearly needed no help. One of her captors had been riddled by Troy's fire, and she had seized the opportunity to neutralize the other rebel. She stood over his still body holding his weapon. The green alien officer was nowhere to be seen.

"Hey yourself," she said, sounding every bit as sore as her battered face suggested. Still, she managed to smirk back behind her split lip. "Good timing."

"Kill them!" shouted a voice from behind a nearby collection of shipping containers. The aline officer. "Kill them now!"

All the rebels within earshot turned and leveled their rifles at Sam and Sola, even as they hid behind whatever they could find to stay out of Troy and Bean's scorching fire.

"Move!" shouted Sam.

As he and Sola zipped toward the vehicles, traces of blaster fire smacked the earth behind them. It would only take a second before one of those bolts found its target. They weren't going to make it.

But ahead of them, Fenra appeared on top of a truck holding a compact anti-personnel grenade launcher. The huge weapon looked almost like a toy on her massive shoulder. With a roar she sent two rocket-assisted grenades zipping through the air, leaving a thin line of white smoke in their wake.

Shrapnel flew at the rebel forces, who dove for cover.

The enemy fire subsided, but it didn't go away completely. Yellow blaster fire still charred the ground all around them.

Sam suddenly felt like someone had shoved a burning hot poker in his left butt cheek, through his armor and into his skin. He'd been hit.

He stumbled, but Sola grabbed him, keeping him from falling. "C'mon, Leej!"

They were close to Troy and Bean's position. Troy had nearly depleted his belt of ammunition, but his rate of fire didn't slow. "Get some!" he screamed.

A chest-thumping explosion knocked both Sola and Sam to the ground. Sam quickly shook off his disorientation, gave himself a once-over, and began crawling toward Sola on hands and knees.

"You all right?" Bean asked over L-comm.

"Yeah. Grenade?"

"Close one!"

Sola, who didn't have the luxury of Legion armor, was fishing a piece of shrapnel from her bleeding arm. She yanked out a two-centimeter-long sliver of metal, causing her blood to flow even more freely. Sam quickly pulled a skinpack from his webbing and slapped it over the wound. Sola didn't make so much as a whimper during the entire ordeal, brief though it was.

Sam pulled her to her feet, and the two of them ran the remaining twenty yards to the truck.

"I'm out!" Troy shouted over comm. "Gonna fire up the engines and get us out of here!"

But before he'd even finished talking, Fenra leaped across a vehicle, landed just in front of the truck, and darted into the driver's seat. A second later, the decrepit combustion engine roared to life. Either someone had left the keys in the ignition, or Fenra hotwired the thing like a professional car thief. Sam guessed the latter was more likely.

"Get in, get in!" Bean shouted between bursts on the blaster cannon.

Sam shoved Sola into the back of the truck, but as he attempted to follow her, with one foot still on the ground and the other on the bumper, Fenra stomped on the gas. Sam's legs spread into a split, and he found himself holding on and being dragged.

Thankfully Bean caught sight of his predicament and stopped firing long enough to grab Sam's hand and yank him aboard. "I got you, Sarge!"

"Thanks!" Sam picked off a rebel shooter with his newly acquired blaster pistol as he ran to the front of the truck. He slammed a fist on the roof of the cab. "Full speed, Fenra! Don't stop!"

Yellow blaster fire chased the fleeing vehicle like a shower of rain. Its sides were plated against energy weapons, and the blaster bolts ricocheted after a resounding *dunk*—but the men atop the vehicle were not similarly shielded. That vulnerability became instantly apparent when the sound of the blaster cannon ceased and Bean went down with a grunt.

"Bean!" Troy yelled.

Sam turned to see Bean grabbing his shoulder and writhing in pain on the truck bed. "Get on that gun!" he ordered Troy.

Troy was up in an instant, coupling the heavy repeater to a new pack and pulling back the charge engage. He squeezed the trigger and didn't let go, lost in the fog of war. "Come on! Come on!"

"Stop encouraging them!" Sola shouted back.

Fenra drove exactly like you'd expect an eight-foot ly-conlore to drive. She wheeled madly around vehicles and blasted right through everything else in her path, whether supply crates or fleeing rebels. The bouncing and rocking nearly threw Sam out of the pickup bed. It made getting a shot on target exceedingly difficult.

And then she shot out of the camp and sped down a wide jungle supply road.

They weren't out of the woods yet. Despite the chaos at the base, three rebel vehicles were already in pursuit. Still, he took the opportunity to check on his wounded leej.

"Bean! You all right?"

Blood was oozing out of Bean's shoulder. The blaster bolt had sent fragments of his expensive new legionnaire armor through the synthprene undersuit and into his flesh.

Bean looked over at the wound, holding the wounded arm close to his chest. "I'll be fine. Get me back up."

It was clear he was injured far worse than what he was admitting, but Sam understood. Right now, there was no time for a legionnaire to be hurt. If you could fight, you fought.

"My man." Sam yanked Bean to a sitting position.

The truck bounced so hard it sent them all a few inch-es into the air. As they slammed back down on the metal bed, Sam bit his tongue, hard, sending a spray of blood into his mouth.

Sam looked back at the pursuing vehicles. There were three of them, though they were troop transports, not designed to keep up with the lighter technical. Still, their drivers knew these roads, these turns, and they were managing to keep pace. Rebel gunners leaned out passenger windows firing heavy repeater rifles at them. So far, their fire was wild and undisciplined—more of a threat to the clouds than their targets—but all it took was one lucky shot. Bean was proof of that.

Troy's blaster cannon went quiet.

"Get the gun back in the fight!" Sam shouted. He was using his pistol to try and pick off the driver of one of the pursuing trucks—with no success. Fenra wasn't making it easy to line up anything approaching a decent shot.

"About that, Sarge..." Troy said from behind the blaster cannon. "You want the bad news or the worse news? Because there's nothing good in this scenario."

Sam looked up and saw the barrel of the weapon smoking red hot. The conduit connecting it to its charge pack had melted into a plastic slag. "Pretty sure I got an idea about what the worse news is." He shook his head. "All right, help me look through what else is on this truck. Maybe there's something we can use."

It would have been nice if one of those crates or burlap-wrapped bundles contained an aero-precision launcher. Sam was getting tired of wasting blaster depletions on near-impossible shots. If only he had an N-4 with spare packs, those drivers would be full of holes and their trucks would be overturned on the side of the road.

Yeah. Wish in one hand...

"So what was the bad news, then?" Sola asked. She was taking shots at their pursuers with her Raptor 210, and her aim and luck didn't seem to be any better than Sam's.

"That white bar of chow you fed us for breakfast went right through me. I *really* gotta go."

There was something about the absolute seriousness of Troy's delivery that cut through everything for a brief, surreal moment. Bean was the first to laugh, though it was clear the effort pained him. Then Troy began to sputter out quick, snorting laughs of his own. Sola and Sam followed. There were times when the universe went to hell in a coffin and all you could do was laugh.

A yellow blaster bolt struck the top of the cab and dropped a shower of sparks. Fenra swerved, sending everyone sliding to one side. The motion dropped Bean from his propped-up sitting position to the deck, where he stayed.

That snapped them all back to reality.

Sam cracked open a crate containing a green metal case. The case was painted with a black skull and the words, "Caution: Vibro Shields. Do Not Activate Until Removed From Packaging."

"Troy!" he yelled. "Help me get these out!"

Blaster fire scorching the air all around them, they threw back the heavy black clasps and opened the case.

Sam and Troy looked inside, then exchanged a smile.

"Yeah," said Sam. "I think we can use these."

CHAPTER 20

The vibro shields were designed to attach to the wearer's forearm. They were sleek—matte black with a green control system—if a bit bulky. They reminded Sam of some of the older Legion tech.

"You familiar with these?" Troy asked.

"Sort of." Sam picked one up. "Not the name, but it's just a type of vambrace." He slipped one over his left forearm. It fit snugly around the armor. "They fit like this."

Troy lifted one out and attached it. "Why's a shield got three buttons on it?"

"Your guess is as good as mine." Sam scanned the buttons. "But hey, they came in a box with a skull, so they've got to be good."

The buttons were red, blue, and green. Guessing the green button would be the least likely to kill him, Sam pressed it.

A blue, oval energy shield popped up from the vambrace, large enough to cover him from shins to shoulders—and since he wasn't standing up, the bottom of the shield pressed against the truck bed, thrusting his arm up over his head. The thing felt as real and solid as any physical shield Sam had ever come across. On the right side was a square opening where a rifle or blaster could fit.

Troy tapped the green button on his own vambrace, and another shield appeared. "Cool," he said with a broad grin.

On one knee, Sam found he could cover both himself and Sola. Troy did the same for Bean.

"How many grenades we got left?" Sam shouted. "Give what we've got to Sola!"

They'd found the shields at an opportune time. The road smoothed out a bit here, aiding the rebels' aim. A yellow blaster bolt struck Sam's shield directly—and pinged right off. Not so much as a tremor raced up his arm. *These things must have some kind of shock-absorbing feature,* he thought. This was impressive tech. Core-world stuff.

As Sola holstered her blaster and gathered the grenades the leejes handed her, Fenra leaned her head out the window and roared something. Her gray fur pressed against her skull as the wind raced over her.

"What's she saying?" Sam yelled.

"She said we're running out of road!" Sola shouted. "We've got to make this quick!"

Sam didn't dare chance a look over the cab to see just how much time they had. He did, however, notice that the jungle that pressed in on either side was beginning to thin. They had to be closing in on the water.

"Toss those fraggers!"

Yellow blaster fire traced a line across Sam's and Troy's shields, but the bolts dissipated as soon as they made contact. The only aftereffect was a tiny ripple that slowly faded.

"Here we go!" Sola shouted, lobbing the first grenade.

The fragger bounced on the road once, twice, and then got stuck in the grille of the first truck.

Sam's eyes went wide. "Well, what are the odds—"

The grenade exploded. Black smoke lifted to the sky as red and orange flames licked the cab from the engine. The driver swerved wildly, throwing the gunner right over the side. As the vehicle plowed off the road and out of control into the jungle, still trailing flames, the next truck in line rolled right over the helpless gunner.

Already Sola had tossed a second and third grenade. The two resulting explosions enveloped the remaining pursuers in a cloud of shrapnel, shredding tires and perforating fluid lines. The trucks stalled out and slowed. It wasn't as dramatic as what happened to the first truck, but more effective. Those vehicles were dead in the road, blocking any other vehicles that might attempt pursuit.

Fenra stomped on the gas, and they careened around a tight curve. Troy fell against Sam, and when their shields hit one another, they sent a shower of sparks into the air.

"My bad," Troy said, righting himself. He turned to his injured friend. "You going to make it, Bean?"

The legionnaire only lolled his head and let out a weak sigh through his external comm.

They ran out of road about a klick later. Fenra stopped the truck and hopped out. There was no water in sight. Apparently they'd have to walk the rest of the way to the boat.

"Can she help with Bean?" Sam asked Sola, nodding at Fenra.

"You should ask her."

Sam removed his helmet and looked up at the gray-furred creature earnestly. "Will you help us get him back to the ship, Fenra?"

The lyconlore seemed pleased to be asked this. She gave a toothy grin that passed for a smile, then gingerly picked up Bean and hoisted him over one shoulder. The legionnaire's arms and legs dangled limply, and thin droplets of blood dripped off of Bean's gauntleted hand.

Sola jumped from the truck and jogged into the jungle vegetation. "I'll get the boat fired up. Fenra knows the way."

"What should we do with these?" Troy asked, gesturing to the crate of vambraces.

There was no way Sam was leaving these behind. Not after he'd witnessed how useful they could be under direct fire. He grabbed one side of the heavy green box.

"Ugh! This thing weighs a ton," he grunted.

"Sarge, these things can fit on our arms. They can't weigh that much."

"Yeah, well, the case they're in must be made of dura-crete then."

He hopped off the back of the truck, and together he and Troy pulled the heavy case to the truck's tailgate. As Sam was debating whether to bring the whole case or to just grab whatever they could move quickly with, Fenra stepped up beside them and, with Bean still dangling from her massive shoulder, lifted the case as if it weighed no more than a white meal bar.

"Whoa." Sam shook his head in disbelief at Fenra's strength. "You sure you can hump all that back to the boat?"

The lyconlore hooted an affirmative and set off on the path Sola had blazed.

Troy stretched his back. "If I was eight feet tall and weighed five hundred pounds, I'd be able to lift it too. Just sayin'."

As they followed Fenra through the jungle, Sam kept his blaster in hand. His charge pack wasn't completely spent, but it was close. He'd have to be extremely careful in his decision-making.

Soon the sound of the decrepit boat's engines thrummed from up ahead, followed by Sola's voice.

"Let's go! Let's go!" she shouted. "We got company!"

They tore through the undergrowth and sprinted right into the cold river water, sloshing wildly toward the boat as if being chased by more monk eels. Looking over his shoulder, Sam saw a cloud of dirt being kicked up *very* close by. Someone was coming. The rebels must have cleared the roadblock—or managed a way around it through the jungle itself.

Fenra tossed the case of vambraces inside the boat before hauling herself up with one hand while cradling Bean in the other like a mother carrying her young. Once on board, she extended a paw to Sam, who accepted it with a silent prayer of thanks to the tech in his helmet that filtered out things like the scent of wet lyconlores.

A high-pitched whine sounded from the jungle as a large, beat-up industrial vehicle on repulsors came crashing through the trees. It held two extending arms out in front of it, with a high-powered laser between them, and that beam was cutting through the jungle vegetation like a wire through cheese, toppling trees and cutting down bushes.

Sola backed the boat out of its makeshift dock and slammed the throttle on full. Trucks arrived right on the heels of the jungle thresher, and rebels poured out.

Sam dropped three of them with three well-aimed shots. That was all his charge pack had left. "Anybody got any more grenades?"

Fenra reached into her fur and threw him a black grenade with an old-fashioned pin and depressor.

"I'm not even going to ask where you pulled this from," Sam said.

He yanked the pin and lobbed the grenade. It sailed in a perfect arc and landed in the midst of a clump of rebels kneeling down to fire at them from the riverbank. The explosion eviscerated them and sent several more scattering back into the jungle, or leaping into the river, to avoid any subsequent attacks. They didn't know that was the legionnaires' last grenade, and there wasn't time for them to find out. Sola was already coaxing the *Hawk* downriver, and in seconds they were beyond the reach of enemy weapons fire.

Sam immediately went to check on Bean. Troy was already with him. Both of the legionnaires had removed their helmets, and twin sheets of sweat covered their faces. Across Bean's was a look of controlled pain. Sam was just happy to see the man was conscious.

"I wish we had something to give you, brother," Sam said, crouching down and taking another look at the wound. There was no way of knowing how bad it really was until Bean was out of kit. "We'll be back soon, and Doc will you fix you right up."

"Oh yeah, you'll get the good stuff," Troy said, grinning. "Sometimes I just want to hurt myself to get some. Not— not that I would ever actually do that, Sarge."

"You've got problems, Troy," Sam said.

CHAPTER 21

Sam stood with Captain Zeno and Private Moon in their informal "briefing room"—actually just a corner of the palace grounds near the front gate. The trip back had taken all day, and once again the sun was falling below the horizon. Sam's stomach growled with pure determination that food would be in its immediate future.

"What did it look like exactly?" Private Moon asked with large eyes. The leej tech had grown agitated upon hearing Sam's report. "I mean, I need dimensions, anything that looked familiar. Was it energy-powered or some older technology?"

"I'm telling you all I saw," Sam repeated, frustrated.

He'd reported to Captain Zeno the moment they'd returned to Noi, and though he knew this debriefing was of primary importance, he wanted to be with Troy and Bean, making sure the wounded leej would be all right.

Captain Zeno took control of the discussion. "It was a massive cannon, large enough for Sergeant Samson to fit inside. Big enough that it required disassembly in order to be moved."

Sam offered a bit of speculation. "If I had to guess... I'd say it was energy-powered."

"Why would they want to transport a weapon like that here?" Moon asked.

"Why do you think?" Sam shot back, a bit more acidly than he'd intended.

"Something as big as what Sergeant Samson is describing," Captain Zeno said, rubbing the side of his jaw, "is very bad news. Hard to defend a city when the attacking force is capable of just bringing it all to the ground—which they've already shown they're willing to do. We'll have to make it our main priority to neutralize it, or our objective is already lost."

He paused, considering. "They'll have to reconstruct it somewhere. That'll be our best chance. We take it out on arrival to that location or as it's being built. I'll see about putting together some scouts to catch it early. By the time it's here, it'll already be too late."

Sam nodded. "Agreed, sir."

"Good. Now it's our turn to fill you in, Sergeant." Captain Zeno faced the tech. "Moon, tell Sergeant Samson what you told me about the rebel's bio-weapon."

"Yes, sir," Moon said. "I—"

"And make it the short version, Private."

Moon nodded. "Right. The short version. Well... basically, I've figured out how to operate the weapon, and I've extracted a bit of the gas form of the chemical and tested it. Our buckets will filter it out. We'll be safe."

"Wait," Sam said, confused. "Safe from what? Are you—we're not seriously considering *using* the thing?"

"I have President Gen evacuating the city now," Captain Zeno said with a morbid look in his one good eye. "We'll show them just how much the Legion can KTF. I swear to Oba I'm going to send more than my share of those rebel scum to their graves."

Sam had never witnessed this darker side of the captain. He wasn't sure what to say.

"You're dismissed, Private Moon," Captain Zeno said. "Thank you."

"Sir!" Moon said with a sharp salute and walked away.

Captain Zeno crossed his arms and looked over the palace courtyard where the Cononga militia trained under the watchful eye of two legionnaires. "You did well, Samson. You got the intel we needed and your men back in one piece."

That was technically true, but Sam didn't feel particularly good about what had happened to Bean under his watch. "Doc's looking after Private Rivera now," he said. "I should go check in on him."

"Soon." Captain Zeno turned his gaze from the courtyard to Sam. "You estimated four hundred rebels?"

"Maybe a little more. Definitely not less." Sam let the report hang in the air before adding, "Sir, their weapons worry me more than the number, and not just that big cannon. They're equipped with military-grade rifles and armor. They have grenades. They're not Legion capable, but against the Cononga militia…"

"Four hundred well-armed rebels against two hundred poorly trained Cononga militia would be a slaughter, but four hundred well-armed rebels against two hundred poorly trained Cononga militia *and* the Iron Wolves..." Captain Zeno gave a twisted grin. "I like our odds, Sergeant. Even if we are fighting with weapons left over from the Savage Wars."

"What are the chances the militia just break and run when the fighting gets bloody?" Sam asked. It was a question that had been bothering him since they decided to take on the fight. "Because four hundred against *just* the Iron Wolves... you can't like *those* odds, sir."

"All men are capable of great things when their homes are threatened."

There was a grim knowing in the captain's voice. Like he'd experienced such things first-hand.

Sam waited a beat to see if his captain had anything more to add before saying, "Sola estimates that the rebels could arrive outside the city by tomorrow night if they started marching on our heels. Maybe the next morning if we're lucky."

Captain Zeno nodded. "That'll give me plenty of time to show you what Privates Biel and Hall have pulled together. I'm impressed. They had to get creative, but they pulled it off. Weapons for everyone. They vary widely—no swapping of charge packs or ammo if things get dire—but no one's fighting empty-handed."

"I'm glad to hear it, sir."

"Get some hot chow and then meet me in the palace museum. I want your help getting the squad optimized for defense."

"Yes, sir." Sam wanted only one thing more than to run off and find food. "Permission to visit Rivera first?"

"Certainly." Captain Zeno looked out to the horizon, behind which the sun had just dropped. "I'll meet you there in an hour and ten."

"Thank you, sir."

Sola and Fenra stood waiting by the palace's entrance. Even at a distance, with his helmet off, Sam could smell the lyconlore's rank fur at full force. His eyes watered.

Sola smiled as he approached. "Why are you crying?" she asked. "Bean is going to pull through."

"No—I'm not—it's just..." Sam took a chance and placed a hand on Fenra's hulking shoulder. The big lyconlore didn't recoil or show any aggression. "I'm saying this as a friend, Fenra. You really need to do something about your personal hygiene. Something more than filing your nails into daggers. A bath. Better yet, maybe some kind of chemical wash."

Fenra looked down at Sam with predatory yellow eyes. Her expression made it abundantly clear that she could squash him in a heartbeat.

Sam questioned the wisdom of his actions. Keenly aware that his hand was still on her shoulder, he quickly pulled it away.

Finally, Fenra bared her sharp teeth in a snarling grin and growled something.

"She says she'll take it under consideration," Sola said with a laugh. "But that she *likes* the smell."

"Right," Sam said, awkwardly clapping his hands in front of him. "So... you two evacuating with the rest of the civilians? Captain Zeno said the president ordered the city to be emptied."

"We're not going anywhere," Sola said, patting the Raptor 210 on her hip. "This little baby wants to be the last thing a few more rebels hear before they enter the next life."

"Really?" Sam spoke without thinking. "Did the president offer you more money or something?"

Sola's demeanor immediately changed. Her face formed a furious scowl that rivaled one of Captain Zeno's. "You think all this is to me is *money*?"

Fenra wisely tiptoed away, shaking her head at Sam in disappointment.

Sam knew better than to answer a question phrased like that. So he just waited.

"Some of us *would* fight for the money," Sola said. "Not all of us have our meals taken care of, but that's not me. I'm staying for these people. *My* people, who would be ruled by a dictator if someone doesn't stand up and fight. It's about stopping bullies who think they can get whatever they want if enough bodies lie bloodied in their wake."

Sam held up his hands. "I didn't mean it like that." He tried desperately to think of the right words. "I didn't know you felt so strongly about this. It was wrong of me to assume. I'm sorry."

Sola slowly unclenched her fists. "No, I'm sorry. I… overreacted." She looked out at the dimming horizon. "I need sleep, and Fenra *does* need a bath. She's giving me a headache. Props to you for telling her that and living, by the way. She decapitated the last person who brought up the way she smelled."

Sam wasn't sure if that was true, but he believed it was certainly plausible.

"Anyway, I'm going to grab some sleep," Sola said. "I'll see you around."

There was a brief moment when Sam felt he could say something more. A moment when his eyes caught hers and the possibility of what could be flashed between them, but Sergeant Samson was a legionnaire first and an Iron Wolf last, and the in-between had room for nothing except KTF.

"Sleep well," he said.

CHAPTER 22

"I can do it without the pain meds, Doc. I'm telling you."

Bean hadn't stopped hectoring Doc Dobson about his tolerance for pain, despite the charred red piece of flesh that used to be his shoulder.

Doc pointed an accusing finger at his patient. "You shut up. You came in here half-alive at best, and your arm has so many pieces of armor jutting from it that it looks like the back end of a wormump."

Bean rolled his eyes, looking at Sam for an assist. "Sergeant, tell him to save the meds for someone who really needs it when the fighting starts. I'm good, man. Don't feel nothin'."

Sam shrugged. "His loss, right, Doc?"

Dobson frowned, but he set down the packet of numbing gel. "Fine, but at least take a few swallows of this Conongan rice wine to dull things. Pulling all these fragments out isn't exactly going to tickle."

Bean chugged down several large gulps from the proffered canteen. He was clearly not at all averse to *this* kind of numbing agent.

"Take it easy, Private Rivera," Sam said, sitting down at the edge of his bed. "I don't want you drunk, or hung over, when the fighting starts."

Bean pulled the canteen away from his lips and let out a satisfied sigh. "My tolerance for pain is equaled only by my tolerance for alcohol, Sarge."

Sam smiled, then turned to Dobson. "How's it look?"

Forceps in hand, Dobson moved in to remove the first shard of ruined armor. "A wound like this would definitely get him a Purple Heart. Not gonna put in for the Order of the Centurion, though. He'll be all right."

"I already got a Purple Heart," Bean said.

Dobson gave a wry smile. "What Iron Wolf doesn't?" He plucked out a nasty-looking shard of splintered armor.

"Ow!" shouted Bean.

"I told you!" Dobson chided, patting a fresh flow of blood with an absorb-cloth.

Bean composed himself. "No, it's fine, keep going. Just... surprised me is all."

"Uh-huh." The doctor pulled another piece from Bean's battered shoulder. This time the legionnaire only grimaced.

While he waited, Sam decided to try the local rice wine. He tilted the canteen back, taking a big mouthful— then sprayed the liquid across the room.

"Watch it, Sergeant!" Dobson shouted. "This is supposed to be a sterile operating room."

"Sorry." Sam grimaced. "That's horrible. It tastes like the back end of a skunk rat. It's like some kind of punishment."

Bean was grinning now despite Doc going back to work on his shoulder. "You should see your face, Sarge!" He laughed and grimaced at the same time. "Poor Troy, you sprayed that stuff all over his bunk!"

"Well, blame it on Doc for bringing that garbage into my presence."

"Thanks," muttered Dobson.

Sam rose from his seat, the canteen still in his hand. "I'm going to grab some chow, then check on our makeshift armory. I'll see you Wolves later."

Still focusing on his patient, Dobson said, "Chow's set up in the kitchen. Two rights and your first left from here."

Sam nodded and moved for the door.

"And stay away from the gray stuff!" Dobson called after him. "It tastes worse than what's in that canteen you're stealing."

"Thanks for the tip," Sam said as he left the room.

He heard Bean's voice fading behind him. "Did you see his face when he spit that out? It was the funniest thing since Troy lit himself..."

As Sam followed Doc's directions to the chow, he lifted the canteen to his lips and took a long swig. Yeah, it tasted awful, and it felt like fire racing down his throat, but liquor was liquor, and he'd had worse. The Legion showed you the galaxy... and all the sundry drinks it had to offer.

Two more swigs and Sam was feeling a little light-headed. He kicked himself for failing to follow his own advice. *Time to stop. You're being too damn impulsive. Again.*

The kitchen was a massive room with rolling tables set with cutlery. A pantry to one side was stuffed with enough food to feed an army. Certainly enough to satiate a squad of hungry Iron Wolves.

"No! No! That's not right at all!"

The voice belonged to Lyn, who, Sam was amused to see, was sporting a white apron. He was giving instruction to a broad-shouldered chef with a stern demeanor.

"We need food ready around the clock," Lyn said. "Legionnaires are hungry at all hours of the day." He spotted Sam and waved him over. "Case in point—here is Sergeant Samson. He's here *now* and he needs food before he goes back out there. I need meals that are quick and easy for these men. They're fighting for *you*, after all."

The chef nodded and stepped away to bark orders at his crew.

Sam was impressed to see the Senate liaison pitching in in this way—especially considering he was aiding a cause he knew was neither authorized nor desired by the Republic. Maybe Sam had misjudged the man.

"We'll have something for you in a moment, Sergeant," Lyn said. He paused, raised an eyebrow, and gave Sam a wry smile. "Are you quite all right, Sergeant Samson? Have you been drinking?"

"I'm fine." Sam put the canteen down. He was more hungry now than thirsty anyway. "But I really don't have much time. I have to meet the captain."

"Of course." Lyn gestured for Sam to take a seat. "It really will be hardly any time at all."

"Thanks," Sam said. He eased himself down onto a stool. "You surprise me, Lyn. How come you're so calm about all this?"

"All of what?"

"Breaking direct orders of the Senate, and all the penalties that come with it. I always figured you for a Senatorial yes-man." Sam blurted out the reply more bluntly than he'd meant to. He really should have taken it easier on the alcohol.

"*Well*," said Lyn, sounding as though he'd expected this conversation to come up for some time—and had rehearsed his part of it in front of a mirror at least half a dozen times—"I do work for the Senate, not the *House of Reason*." He said this last bit with an obvious undercurrent of disdain. "And I'm a representative, not a 'point.' I'm in this line of work because, believe it or not, I actually care what happens to these planets on the fringe of the galaxy."

Sam wasn't sure he bought all that, but there was no need for him to reply one way or the other. Lyn was on a roll, excitedly going on about the history of the Republic's successful folding of new worlds into its collective...

The chef reappeared with a broad smile and a bowl of noodles mixed with some kind of meat, vegetables, and sauce.

"Thanks," Sam said. He grabbed a two-pronged fork from the table and stabbed a piece of quivering pink meat almost the instant it was served to him. The meat oozed where the prongs had skewered it, and it slid back off into the pile of shining noodles. "... I think."

Sam dug in despite his reservations about the pink meat—he'd eat anything put in front of him as long as it wasn't moving, and if it *was* still moving, he'd eat that too. He'd just kill it first.

The chef stood by, wringing his hands in anticipation as Sam chewed. Flavors exploded in his mouth like fireworks at a Republic Day celebration. The dish was a perfect mix of sweet and spicy.

"This is great," he said, looking up at the chef with a grin, noodles hanging from his mouth.

The chef positively beamed. "I'm glad you like it. It is a great honor to serve a member of the Iron Wolves." He turned to a rolling serving cart and poured Sam a large glass of amber liquid. "Dragon juice. Please drink."

Sam eyed the tall glass suspiciously before deciding to jump right in. "You haven't done me wrong yet."

The chef watched Sam down the entire glass and then gave him a refill before returning to work with an unmistakably content smile.

Sam realized that throughout this exchange, Lyn had not for a moment ceased talking. He had apparently moved on from Republic history to his innermost thoughts—namely his heavy heart about the current situation. Sam wondered if the man was going to go ahead and have himself a good cry right on the spot.

Bleeding hearts.

"If it were up to *me*," Lyn said, "I'd have had Cononga sign the document right away. I'd have the entire Legion here to give them support, but of course, the president wanted to wait for the official ceremony to sign, and now my orders are the same as yours."

"Yeah, and you're obeying them about as well as I am."

"Oh, no!" Lyn said, as if scandalized by the idea that he was not following orders. "I haven't done anything outside of my operating parameters. Though I want to. Desperately. I want to *help* these people, and yet we're supposed to be standing down, waiting to see what happens, and we both know what will happen." He looked around and lowered his voice. "These people can't stand up to what's coming. What am I supposed to do?"

"Looks like you're already doing it," Sam said through a mouthful of food. "You've already made your choice, but you don't see it yet."

"What do you mean?"

"You said you haven't done anything to violate your mission parameters? Then tell me when you linked up with Major Roy to let him know what Captain Zeno is planning."

Lyn's face went pale. He stepped back, clearly worried that a physical confrontation was forthcoming. "No! I never did that. I would never—"

"Relax," Sam said, slurping up a noodle. He could go for another bowl or two of this stuff. "I know you haven't. That's my point. You're *supposed* to prevent something like what we're doing from happening, but here you are, actually helping us. Before long you'll be grabbing a weapon to defend these people."

"What? Me?" Lyn shook his head. "No, I'm no soldier. I don't know how to fight."

"You'll find a way," Sam said, a prophet speaking to a land on the brink of war. He scooped up the last of his meal. It was time to go. "Where I come from, we have a saying: 'A man can't live with each foot in a different world.' I was wrong about you, Lyn. When it comes down to it, you'll do what you can to help us. I know it."

Lyn's mouth hung open as if he were trying to wrap his mind around this revelation.

"I'll leave you to think about that," Sam said, standing. He held out his empty bowl. "Hey, you think I can get another bowl to go?"

CHAPTER 23

"After we run through the weapons check, we have a strategy briefing with President Gen and Colonel Minh," Captain Zeno said. He gave Sam a level stare. "And then I need you to get a shower and get some rest."

"Sir?"

That hardly seemed like a priority to Sam. Not with all that needed to be done to prepare for the rebels' attack.

"You need the sleep, Sergeant, and the rest of us need you to take a shower. You smell part-lyconlore."

Sam grinned. He was filthy from head to foot, his skin streaked with sweat and his armor streaked with everything from mud to blood. "Sir, not to disobey orders, but I'd rather not sleep after I clean up. The city defenses are going to need a lot of help."

The truth of it was, Sam didn't want to go back to sleep. The nightmare was there, lurking, waiting. He could feel it. He was prepared to swear off sleeping ever again.

"I'm not asking you," Captain Zeno said. "The Conongan militia is more than capable of helping with the city defenses while Sergeant Samson grabs a few hours' rest. Now, Biel and Hall are waiting for us."

Captain Zeno led Sam into the underground museum turned makeshift armory. It looked a lot different than the last time Sam saw it. Stacks of weapons, cleaned and sorted, sat in open crates, as did ammo dumps marked by weapon type. Grenades had their own section, beside a pedestal that held a single brick of ancient plastic explosive, looking like an offering to the old gods of boom. Even the green case of vibro shields was here, and Biel and Hall each had a vambrace on.

"All right, Wolves," Captain Zeno said. "What do you have for us?"

"Sir, let's start with these things," Biel said, modeling his vambrace. "They are beyond cool. The green button activates the shield, the red turns it off, and the blue button... well, Hall can show you."

Hall activated his shield, then grinned as he pressed the blue button. The shield hummed a little faster, and its edges thinned out to sharp-looking points of energy. "It seems whoever designed these beauties kept in mind the need for offense as well as defense."

"You think they'll do all right for hand-to-hand fighting?" Zeno asked.

"Oh, they'll do more than all right. Check this out." Hall motioned for the legionnaires to follow him to an empty wooden crate. He swiped down with the humming vibro shield, striking the box. The shield not only cut right through the box, it even bit into the floor.

"Easy there, Hall," said Sam, but he was impressed.

"No joke," Hall said, turning off his shield. "We'll have to be careful when we use them in this mode, but we'll be able to do some serious damage up close. Only trouble is, they drain a lot of power and probably won't last long in a protracted fight. Not only that, but the charging stations weigh a ton. Biel and me could barely lift the case."

"Then make sure they're all fully charged before the fight," Captain Zeno said. "Show me what else we've got."

Biel once again took the lead. "Almost everything we have is from the Savage Wars." He pointed to various crates as he spoke. "Closest thing to modern tech are some N-1s. Packs a punch, but uses an incompatible charge pack and chews through 'em real quick. Suffers from loss of accuracy at long range. Then we got these heavy repeaters that shoot actual *bullets*. A bunch of fraggers—old-school, but the tech is pretty much the same—and some early blaster-tech sidearms, mostly Raptor two-tens and Jager one thousands."

He came to a stop at the end of the hall at the entryway to an adjoining room. "We'll be able to arm everyone, but in all honesty we'll probably want to let some of those rebels get close enough that we can pick up their weapons after we dust 'em."

"Show them the cool stuff," Hall urged. "The hand-to-hand weapons."

Biel smiled and led them to a corner of the next room. A tall wooden cabinet stood next to an ancient Iron Wolf flag. "President Gen put out a request for the locals to bring any weapons they could spare for the cause. The results were unexpected."

The two privates each took a handle of the cabinet to pull it open. Inside were stacks of swords, spears, axes, and war maces. The kinds of weapons Sam had only seen in pictures—or in specialty shops as souvenirs.

"Badass, huh?" said Hall.

"It'll have to do." Captain Zeno picked up a long, curved sword with a leather-wrapped grip. "If it comes down to hand-to-hand combat, we'll be grateful to have these. Paired with those vibro shields and our armor, we might hold our own when we get overrun."

It didn't slip past Sam that the captain had said "when," not "if."

"It won't be pretty," Biel said, setting someone up for the second half of the mantra the Iron Wolves had used for centuries.

"But it will be victory," Sam finished.

His eye was drawn to a huge weapon with a stone hammer on one end and a steel axe head on the other. A leather strap was affixed, allowing the wielder to hang it over their shoulder, on their back. Unable to resist, he picked it up. It was heavier than he expected. He squared his feet for balance, backed up, and swung the hammer end through the air. It felt good in his hands. Great, actually.

"We can set that baby aside for you if you'd like, Sarge," Hall said, watching Sam like a proud father.

"No, it's okay." Sam put the hammer back with the other weapons. "Let the men take first pick so they're comfortable with what they've got. I'll make do with whatever's left. Even my bare hands, if that's what needs doing."

"Oorah," said Biel. "That's how we KTF."

"You two have done well," Captain Zeno said with an approving nod. He placed the curved sword back with the others. "The sergeant and I are on our way to a meeting with President Gen, but once we have our battle plan in place, I'll send the men down for you to distribute weapons."

"Roger that, sir."

Hall and Biel saluted.

Zeno returned the salute, and he and Sam left the armory and made their way toward the presidential reception room.

"Thoughts before we get there?" Captain Zeno asked Sam. "How do you see the rebels attacking?"

"They're not scared," Sam said, thinking about the green alien commander who he imagined would lead the rebels into battle. "They're set on coming at us guns blazing. We can use that."

"Agreed," Zeno said, licking his lips. "The Iron Wolves will have to take the brunt of the blow, with the Conongan militia filling in the gaps."

"Any word from Major Roy?" Sam couldn't help but ask. "Not that whatever he has to say would sway my actions."

"Nothing. I'm expecting a comm transmission any time now, telling us to return to the ship and leave the Conongans to die. Of course, my comms are down. Must be all this damned humidity, eh, Sergeant?"

"I was thinking the exact same thing, sir." Sam cracked a grin. "We're doing the right thing. For once, we're staying to do the right thing."

The door to the reception room was open, so Sam and Zeno walked inside. President Gen and Colonel Minh were already there, speaking in hushed whispers and looking grim.

"Ah, Iron Wolves," President Gen said, rising to his feet to welcome the two legionnaires. "You again honor us with your presence."

"You two look like you're bursting with good news," Captain Zeno said, eyeing the men. "Anything we should know?"

"It's the rebel army." President Gen took on a pained look Sam had seen in men's eyes before. It was the look of defeat. "It seems they've hired an off-planet mercenary group to bolster their ranks. Captain, we aren't a fighting people. You cannot sacrifice your life, and the lives of your men, for a battle we can't win. I—"

"You don't get to make that decision for us." Captain Zeno stalked toward the president with so much intensity that Sam thought he might attack the Conongan leader. "My men and I decided to stay and fight because we owed it to ourselves to do what we felt was right. To do what the Legion was founded to do."

This impromptu speech, brief as it was, seemed to inspire Colonel Minh, who rose proudly to his feet and puffed out his chest.

Zeno gave the colonel a nod of acknowledgment before returning his gaze to the president. "President Gen, spit the taste of defeat from your mouth and tell us the hard facts. Who, exactly, is coming for us?"

"Not who." President Gen looked half terrified, half ashamed. "What."

Captain Zeno didn't miss a beat. "Okay then, *what* is coming for us?"

It was Colonel Minh who answered, though his new-found courage seemed to fade as he spoke. "The rebels have bought the services of a mercenary sectoid hive. They'll be here in hours. We have... no way of stopping them."

CHAPTER 24

Sam ran through everything he knew about the sectoids. They were an alien race, humanoid but insectile, hence the name. More bug than man, they had large eyes, a dense exoskeleton, and antennae. They fought with plasma blasters as well as blades that sprang from their forearms.

He hadn't seen any of these creatures on reconnaissance.

"How could those backwater rebels afford sectoids?" he asked, again speaking his mind without a filter, but the question was valid. No one on the planet seemed particularly wealthy. Then again, the rebels had somehow found a way to obtain some costly weaponry. There were clearly some deep pockets behind this backwater force.

President Gen's face curled into a derisive snarl. "It is Topkin and Hu—the nations north and east of us. I am certain they are the ones aiding the rebels. All on this planet fear my being the first to join the Republic. They know it will only be a matter of time until the planet unites as one Cononga and joins the rest of the galaxy."

"So much for trying to find that cannon before they arrive," Sam said dryly.

"How many of these sectoids are we talking about?" Captain Zeno asked.

"My scouts report an enemy force of three hundred to four hundred strong," Minh said. "Captain, perhaps... perhaps our focus should be on leaving the city. This fight is over before it has even begun."

"Over? Nothing's over!" Captain Zeno glared at the colonel. "It's over when *we* say it's over. I don't want to hear you speak like that again—not to me, not to your men, not even to yourself. You get me, soldier?"

Colonel Minh stood straighter and nodded.

"Say it," Captain Zeno growled. "I want to hear you *say* it!"

"We won't give up," Colonel Minh said.

"Louder!"

"We won't give up. *I* won't give up!" Minh shouted. And he actually sounded like he meant it.

"Good." Captain Zeno rolled his shoulders. "Now. Get me a map of the city so we can get ready to meet these walking corpses."

Minh rushed from the room.

"Captain, a word?" Sam asked.

Captain Zeno nodded, and the two leejes stepped out of earshot of the president.

"You know I'm with you to the end," Sam said quietly. "My men won't back down either. We won't give up here, but what Minh said... I'm just—well, I don't know what I'm saying. I guess I just wanted to make sure we're on the same page here."

"And what page is that, Sergeant?"

"That what we're planning to attempt is crazy."

Captain Zeno sniffed. "Yeah, I think that's the correct page, but we're all crazy, Sam. We're legionnaires. And we're entering a shooting war soon. I need to put together a plan, and I need you to make sure the men understand it, Sergeant."

"Yes, sir. That shower and sleep will have to wait a bit longer."

"So it will."

Colonel Minh ran back into the room with a paper map of the city. The others gathered around as he spread it out on the table. Sam shook his head at the use of paper. *This place is stuck so far in the past,* he thought, *that archaeologists searching for clues about the Ancients might just want to ask the Conongans what they personally remember.*

"The sectoid force is coming from the north," Colonel Minh said, pointing to a spot on the map. "They'll hit us there, and if they don't kill us, the rebels will. Two waves of forces, each about four hundred strong."

"We'll let them reach the city," Captain Zeno said. "Then we'll make them pay for every inch." His one good eye roved around the map, and he tapped at a few different spots. "This is our first fallback point. Here's the second. Casualty collection here. We make the palace our last stand. Sergeant?"

"Yes, sir. I'll tell the men. We should go soon."

"Agreed." Captain Zeno looked to Minh. "Get your militia to the palace courtyard in ten minutes, geared and ready to go. If you need more weapons, see Hall and Biel down in the museum. Sergeant Samson?"

"Yes, sir?"

"Assemble the Wolves."

CHAPTER 25

News of the mercenary invasion force traveled through the palace grounds like wildfire. Sam traveled even faster, and in minutes he'd found all the Iron Wolves and ordered them to report to the armory immediately.

The men were full of questions when they arrived, still pulling on their armor.

"Dude, what's going on?" Jarman asked as Sam handed out the vibro shields. "I thought we had another day or so before the fun started."

"Captain Zeno will explain everything once he gets here," Sam said. He knew better than to break the news to the unit before Zeno had the chance to put it first in his own words. "Right now, gear up for a fight."

"So," Thompson said, inspecting his gear, "I'm going into a fight with a sniper rifle, a vibro shield, three grenades, a knife, and an ancient sword?" He grinned from ear to ear. "I *like* this planet."

"How do these things work again?" Doc Dobson asked as he screwed with the vambrace on his forearm. "The blue button turns the edges to blades?"

"Green on, red off," Sam said, pressing the buttons on his own vibro shield to show the others. "Blue makes it stabby."

"Iron Wolves!" Captain Zeno barked as he stalked into the armory. "Let me hear an oorah!"

"Oorah!" Every legionnaire stood at attention.

"Keep gearing up," Captain Zeno shouted. "I only need your ears right now, not your eyes." As he spoke, he strapped on a vibro shield, one of the N-1s, and the same curved sword he'd held before. The hilt of the sword stuck up over his right shoulder. "Reliable intelligence reports a sectoid mercenary group about to hit the city. It seems the rebels realized the Iron Wolves are protecting Noi and opened their wallets to get some help." He grabbed a seven-inch knife and placed it in a thigh holder on his right leg. "I'm going to go give the Conongan militia a pep talk, but I wanted to talk to you all separately."

Nine pairs of eyes looked to their leader. Bean was there despite his shoulder, standing next to Troy. Hall and Biel were passing out ammunition. Moon and Doc stood next to Jarman and Thompson. None of them had elected to equip the heavy war hammer. Sam picked it up and slung it over his shoulder.

"When we go out there, we're representing more than just the Republic," Captain Zeno said. "We're representing the Legion. More importantly, we're representing the *Iron Wolves*. These people trust the Wolves. They'll be looking to us when things get bad. They'll be looking to the Iron Wolves to hold the line. *And we—will—hold—the—line!*"

"Oorah! Oorah! Oorah!" nine voices shouted back.

"All right then. Let's go to work."

"I want the Wolves standing behind me when I address the Conongan militia in the courtyard," Captain Zeno said to Sam as they jogged up the steps to the first floor. "When we're done, head into the city and start setting up converging fields of fire. We want to use these streets to our advantage. President Gen already had a public works project setting up barricades. Those sectoids try to march through the city, we'll slaughter them."

"What's the plan for the militia itself?" Sam asked.

"I'll have them split into two groups. One to watch our right flank and the other our left. When we get pushed back into the city, we'll lure the enemy in between the two flanks and catch them in another kill box."

"Understood." That would mean the Wolves would be taking the bulk of the enemy fire. It would be their job to make sure the enemy followed them before the trap could be sprung. "After that we'll fight from building to building until we reach the palace?"

"That's the plan."

The men exited the building into a cool crisp night. Cononga's twin moons were high in the sky and provided more than enough light to see by. The courtyard was packed with nearly two hundred Conongan militia, along with President Gen, Colonel Minh, Lyn, Sola, and of course Fenra, towering above the rest.

Sam gave Sola a quick nod, and she shot him a smile in return.

The Iron Wolves lined up beside the Conongan militia. In their armor, they were almost giants compared to the local soldiers, as much as Fenra was to them.

Captain Zeno exchanged a few words with Colonel Minh before stalking up and down in front of the men who would form the city's only defense. He made an imposing figure, almost scowling as he reviewed the men, helmet in one hand and N-1 in the other.

"There are enemies at our doorstep!" he roared, spittle flying from his mouth. "They've come for your homes, they've come for your freedom, they've come for your very lives! In the Legion we have a saying: KTF. It stands for Kill Them First. And that, gentlemen, is exactly what we're going to do."

"Rah!" the Cononga militia bellowed into the night.

"Oorah!" the Iron Wolves screamed back.

"Rah!"

"Oorah!"

The energy that coursed through the air was tangible, and Sam felt his adrenaline building already. The same feeling that always hit him before a battle: one part nervous, one part excited, with fear always lurking.

Colonel Minh ordered his men to move out toward their assigned staging areas. The colonel, Sola, and Fenra joined the captain and Sam.

"We've decided to put Sola and Fenra on the left flank," Colonel Minh said with resolve. "They know the city just as well, if not better, than my own men, and they've seen more fighting. I'll be on the right."

"Good enough for me." Captain Zeno looked a determined Sola, and an intimidating Fenra, up and down. "Make sure your comms are tuned to this channel." He put on his helmet and sent a link-up burst. "If we coordinate this correctly, we'll kill scores of them before they know what hit 'em."

Minh and Sola nodded. Fenra grinned.

Captain Zeno trotted off toward Private Moon. Colonel Minh gave Sam a crisp salute and took off to join his men on the right flank.

"Fenra, did you bathe?" Sam asked with a smile. "You did, didn't you?"

The lyconlore no longer smelled like a garbage can. In fact she smelled quite good. Vanilla and... cinnamon?

Fenra growled something that made Sola chuckle. "Easy with the morbid thoughts, Fen. We're not going to die tonight."

"What'd she say?"

"She says it's a custom of her race to clean oneself before finding a good death in battle." Sola rolled her eyes. "She has a tendency for the dramatic."

Fenra huffed and walked off.

Sam chuckled. "You should convince her she's about to find a good death more often."

Sola grinned and pointed to Sam's new war hammer. "Looks like you've gone all primeval."

"Yeah, well, beggars can't be choosers." Sam eyed Sola's own arsenal. Along with the Reaper 210 that hung low on her hip, she held an ancient N-1 in her hands and a small blade in a holster in her boot. "I see I'm not the only one who raided the palatial museum."

"I plan on doing a lot of killing." Sola looked after Fenra. "Well, I better get going. Keep your head down out there."

"Don't need to. That's why I have one of these." Sam placed his bucket on his head. "KTF, Sola."

"KTF."

CHAPTER 26

Walking through an evacuated city at night was a strange feeling. Abandoned stores and empty homes, without so much as a light in a window, gave the place a shadowy, forlorn feel.

It was a marked contrast with the living, bustling, celebrating city of Noi that Sam had first witnessed, its people turning out to greet the Iron Wolves with ecstatic waves and smiles. He thought once more of the young boy—the one who'd wanted to be an Iron Wolf one day. That innocent boy had been one of the first casualties of this rebellion fostered by some unknown, hostile element. Perhaps it was Topkin and Hu, as the president believed. Perhaps it was the Mid-Core Rebellion. Perhaps something else.

To the boy, what did it matter?

That kid had probably never even had the opportunity to have his first real crush, let alone discover love, and now he never would. He would never be able to find his passion in life. Never would he laugh or cry with his own children. All of that had been taken from him.

Anger rushed over Sam, and molten lava coursed through his dark and violent heart. There was no mercy to be found within him, not for sectoid or rebel. He was ready to kill them all.

He walked along with the rest of the Iron Wolves. Thompson was in the lead, with Captain Zeno, Troy, and Bean bringing up the rear. They were in a section of the city Sam hadn't seen yet. Single-story homes and apartment buildings abounded. Streets were blocked off with walls of debris, furniture, trees, stone—anything the citizens could find before evacuating. Navigating these streets would be like moving through a labyrinth.

It was going to get dirty here. Bloody in a way only building-to-building fighting could be.

As they arrived at the designated location, Zeno spoke over the comms. "Scouts have spotted the first of them. Just their own scouts, still a few clicks out. They're coming right where we expected, so let's hurry and get set up."

"Roger that," Sam said. "Relaying that to the colonel."

He switched from L-comm to a private channel with only Sola and Minh. "Colonel Minh, Sola, we're setting up. Forces are coming where we thought they would. The Wolves are waiting to catch them between a four-story apartment building on the left and a single-story white building with blue trim on the right. It looks like a barber shop or something."

"Understood," Minh said. "I know the place. It's where my father took me to get my hair cut as a boy. We'll set up a block over, ready to take care of anyone who makes it out of the barricades and escapes the kill basket."

"Kill *box*," Sola said. "And it's not a barber shop, it's a grocery store. The barber shop is across from an empty lot.

You need to set up two blocks before where you're thinking, Colonel. I'm setting up the left flank in position now."

"Oh," Minh said, his voice trembling. He'd nearly stranded himself and his soldiers out in front. "Yes, I know where you mean now."

Captain Zeno and Thompson were conversing through a direct comm and pointing out positions. Their helmets hid their faces, but Sam could imagine what they looked like. Captain Zeno was looking hard and determined, and Thompson was grinning wickedly, eager to shoot something.

Zeno came back over the squad's L-comm. "Thompson, I want you up on the roof of that apartment building on overwatch. Jarman, you go with him. Troy, you and Bean get that heavy repeater in the grocery store, and set up deep enough so they don't see it until it's too late!"

"Yes, sir!"

The legionnaires sprinted off. Bean still had the use of only one arm, but he carried what ammunition he could while Troy bore the heavy repeater.

"As for the rest of you Wolves," Zeno said, "we have to be creative given our limited resources. Usually we'd get inside the building and eat them up from the high ground with N-4s and SABs, but we don't have enough charge to keep up a consistent rate of fire, and we can't afford to get trapped inside the apartments. So dig in on either side of the street. Don't use your vibro shields until you need to. Let's get these suckers in nice and close. I want every trigger pull to result in an enemy casualty."

The Iron Wolves rushed to obey their orders. Sam chose a spot on the street immediately below Thompson and Jarman. The first story of the apartment building was surrounded by a privacy wall with a gate of solid steel. As Sam swung the gate open, it emitted a haunted creak that seemed to fill the abandoned city.

"Cut that noise," someone hissed over L-comm.

Sam figured their buckets amplified the creaking, making it sound louder than it actually was, but it *did* sound loud enough to be heard all the way out in the jungle. He took shelter behind the heavy metal gatepost, planning to pivot out and fire through the gaps between bars.

Moon and Doc Dobson hustled past him and took cover behind the wall.

"Mind if we join you?" Doc said.

"Always nice to have a medic close by."

"That's bad luck talk," Moon grumbled.

Zeno came over the L-comm with a report. "Hall and Biel are coming down from their scouting overwatch. Don't open fire."

The two legionnaires ran down the middle of the street and peeled off, setting up opposite Sam. Captain Zeno joined them.

"Never fought sectoids before," Moon breathed. "Wonder what color they bleed."

"We'll be finding out soon enough," Sam said, peeking around the gate.

Moon and Doc set up their own lanes of fire just inside the gate. Their N-1s bristled from behind the wall.

Doc chuckled.

"What's so funny?" Sam asked.

"Oh, nothing," Doc said with a sigh. "You know... the Legion recruiter never mentioned we'd be using ancient Savage Wars weapons, or that our squad sergeant would be setting up an ambush so he could smash some bugs with the war hammer on his back."

"Really? Mine did," answered Sam. "That's the only reason I joined up."

Moon and Doc laughed.

He's right, Sam thought to himself. *You can't write this stuff, but it always boils down to the same thing. Legionnaires out on the edge of the galaxy, ready to kill. Ready to die.*

"I've got eyes on the first group of scouts coming in," Thompson said into the ether of the L-comm. "I see twenty sectoids... no, make that thirty. Looks like light weapons, nothing too wild. I can start dusting 'em as soon as you say, Captain."

"Hold your fire for now," Captain Zeno replied.

The night vision in Sam's bucket picked up the alien mercenaries. They were about two blocks away, picking their way over the piled rubble blockades. The sectoids were tall and slender. A form of natural armor, like a carapace, covered their chests, legs, and arms. No helmets protected their heads, but everything about those alien noggins looked hard—especially the mandible jaws. Their skin—if that's what you could call the parts not covered by the carapace armor—was bright re, and in true mercenary form, they were equipped with a wide assortment of blaster rifles, each sectoid equipping itself to its own liking.

"Easy," Captain Zeno whispered as they came within a block of the Iron Wolves. "No one fires until I give the command."

Sam knew they needed to draw the enemy in, but he felt the captain was really pressing his luck with this one.

The sectoids' antennae twitched as they silently crept forward, as if tasting the night air for an ambush, but if so, they didn't taste the Wolves. They continued forward, right where they were supposed to go, cut off from any side-street exits.

Twenty yards away now. They were so close that Sam could make out every detail of their crimson faces. Black eyes the size of his fists sat atop their oval-shaped heads. Their mouths opened on the sides, with two sharp, pointed mandibles that made a clicking noise as they revealed rows of sharp teeth within a slimy maw.

Sam regretted choosing a crouching position. He should have laid down flat like Moon and Dobson. His muscles burned, screaming at him to move. How snipers managed to hold still for so long was a mystery, but his choice was made, and he'd have to deal with the discomfort.

The sectoids were but a few yards away now—and still completely unaware of the ambush lying in wait. Their antennae seemed to fail them when it came to detecting armored legionnaires lurking in the shadows.

Sam slowed his breathing and aimed down the barrel of his N-1. At this range, even this old beast of a gun would do the job easily.

"Arrrooo!" Captain Zeno howled like a wolfman and began painting the sectoids with red blaster fire.

The captain was an ace shot. Three rounds in rapid fire obliterated a sectoid mercenary's head. Two more rounds ate the face of a second.

Two kills in as many seconds. Got to love the captain.

Sam annihilated his own target with a single shot between the creature's bug-like eyes. *Oorah!*

The scene that had been so quiet just moments before had now erupted into a storm of red blaster fire. Before the Wolves had even swapped out their first charge packs, at least half of the thirty sectoids were down, either dead, or dying.

The remaining sectoids ran for cover, some hugging the walls and doorframes to avoid the funnel of fire, others trying to get small behind toppled dumpsters and other debris. Return fire came in sporadic, wild splatters of blue rounds.

The Wolves picked off target after target.

It was clear the sectoids were panicked. A couple of them left the cover they had found in favor of an all-out sprint back the way they came. These simply died tired.

Sam had his eyes on a doorframe where he knew a sectoid was holed up. He controlled his breathing, pressed another pack into the stock of his weapon, and sighted down the barrel, waiting for a target to appear.

"Easy does it, boys," Captain Zeno said over comms, as calm and cool as ever. "They're not escaping. Conserve your shots and save what charge you've got left. Remember, this was the easy wave. The next time they come through here they'll be expecting us."

A chorus of rogers followed his words as the final sectoids fell in the streets.

"We all clear?" a leej asked over L-comm.

"One more," Sam said, still watching.

The sectoid peeked around the corner, its massive head bobbing like a balloon tied to a doorknob. Sam squeezed his trigger and felt the rough recoil of his weapon hitting his shoulder. The sectoid's head snapped back, and its body slumped forward.

"Pretty sure that was the last one," Sam said.

"All right," Zeno said. "If you're close enough to grab their weapons or ammo safely, do so. The more firepower we have on our side, the merrier."

"Dude, we can do this all night," Moon whispered at Sam's side. "It's like shooting practice targets out here."

Before Sam could respond, Thompson came over the comms. "Hey, we got a problem here. I can see the main sectoid force moving into the city. They're going roughshod over the barricades. It looks like they're... riding monsters."

CHAPTER 27

"I'm gonna need more details than that, Private," Captain Zeno said.

"I'm sorry, sir. That's what they look like." Thompson's voice was strained. "I'd say about a hundred sectoids. Half of 'em riding, um... four-legged armored beetles with huge pincers."

"Flying?"

"No, sir. Riding them over land."

Sam did his best to sound calm, though he didn't relish this new development. "They'll bleed just like everything else. Standard protocol for encountering organics like this: focus fire until we break through their hides or exoskeleton. They'll go down."

"No sense in holding back now," Captain Zeno said. "They know where we are. Grenades as a final welcome, then fall back as needed."

Sam squinted down the street littered with the bodies of the dead sectoids. "Hey Moon," he said, inserting a new charge pack into his N-1 and cracking his neck from side to side. "They bleed green."

"Saw that, thanks."

The sectoid force could be heard before the legionnaires on the lower levels caught visuals. They sounded like a stampeding herd more than a marching enemy. Fear was present in the back of Sam's mind, but it was more of an afterthought, quietly screaming in its assigned corner. If the Legion had taught Sam anything, it was that *he* was the one to be feared.

Do your job.

Stand your ground.

KTF.

A line of sectoid riders came galloping down the street, clearly intent on taking the legionnaires head-on.

"I had a nightmare like this once," Doc said.

"You ain't dreamin', Doc." Sam sighted down the barrel of his weapon, set his jaw, and painted one of the creatures' black skulls as it lumbered forward, indicating to his fellow legionnaires where to fire if they should also open up on his target.

The sectoids opened fire first, filling the street with blue blaster fire. It was clear they didn't have visuals on the hidden legionnaires and were simply hoping to keep them suppressed until they could roll over them.

Sam emptied his pack into his target. All five shots were grouped tightly, four slamming into the beast's skull and one glancing off its pincer, wrenching it off, but the beast didn't go down; its exoskeleton was thicker than Sam had thought. It was hurting, shaking its head with rage, but it kept coming.

Sam slammed in a fresh pack as blue sectoid fire pinged off the gate and scorched the ground beside him.

Thompson and Jarman took a different approach. Firing from above, they dropped the sectoid riders and left the beasts to do whatever.

Sam knew that was the smart call—and still zeroed in on his armored target again. His blood was up, and he was entering that zone—that reckless zone—where he just acted on rage. Like in the office building when Sola had to stop him from beating that alien senseless. Like all the other times that saw him get busted back down to corporal.

He just couldn't help it.

Five more shots rang from his N-1, all of them hitting where he wanted. These Savage Wars weapons really kicked, to the point that Sam thought he might find some bruising on his shoulder, even with the armor on. Legionnaires must have had much heavier plating back in the Savage.

His persistence paid off. The black exoskeleton around the bug's head ripped open like a cracked egg. The bug threw its rider, who was trampled by a trailing beast. Green brain matter poured out of the creature's head as it writhed on the ground.

So—they could be taken down, but not fast enough. Not with the weapons the Iron Wolves had at their disposal.

"Last pack!" Sam shouted as he rammed his last charge into his N-1. He searched the battlefield for another weapon to use, wishing he'd sprinted up the street for one of the sectoids' rifles when he had the chance.

Stupid, Sam. Stupid.

Troy and Bean took down another of the creatures on their side of the street, the heavy repeater rifle keeping up a steady stream that sounded like the constant beat of a drum.

"Troy!" Sam shouted, giving advice that he should have followed himself two charge packs ago. "Don't waste your time on those mounts. Dust the riders!"

"Copy, Sarge!"

"Doc!" Captain Zeno shouted over L-comm. "Hall's hit. We need you over here ASAP."

Sam glanced across the street to see a bloodied Hall propped up behind a building. Biel gripped Hall's hand before leaving to rejoin the fight.

"Roger that," Doc yelled, gathering his equipment and preparing to dart across the blaster-filled avenue. "On my way."

The fire was so thick, Sam didn't see how Dobson would avoid getting hit.

"Moon!" he shouted. "Let's give Doc an escort. Use the vibro shields."

"I thought you'd never ask," Moon said, rising from his stomach and crawling over beside Sam. He pressed the green button on his vambrace, activating the humming, light blue shield. "Let's roll!"

Sam hit the button on his own vambrace. "Doc, follow us!"

The sectoids were closing in, no more than a few dozen yards from overrunning their position.

"Place is getting crowded!" Captain Zeno called. "Grenades!"

The Iron Wolves tossed fraggers among the charging sectoids and their mounts. The series of explosions sent antennae flying and perforated mercenary and beast alike with red-hot shrapnel.

Sam and Moon held up their vibro shields with Doc lobbing grenades over the barrier they created. The trio of legionaries walked slowly but steadily across the street. The blue bolts that found the shields bounced off harmlessly—pebbles tossed by children.

A grenade exploded directly beneath one of the beasts, sending the full force of its blast into its underbelly. The creature stood still, as if unharmed, but its guts spilled out beneath it like someone emptying a bucket.

"Ooh, that's *nasty*!" Moon shouted.

Enemy fire slackened during the barrage of fraggers, but picked up again just as the trio of legionnaires arrived at the other side of the street. Zeno and Biel kept up their fire as Doc knelt down to look at the wounded legionnaire.

Hall was in bad shape. He'd taken a few rounds in his chest plate, and at least one had gotten through.

"He's going to be okay, right?" Biel asked, panic in his voice. He dropped out of the fight and ran over. "He's going to make it. Right, Doc?"

"Give me some room," Doc said. He had to physically push the legionnaire away. "Dammit, Biel! Give me some room!"

"Get that man out of the way and back in the fight, Sergeant!" Captain Zeno ordered while continuing to engage the enemy.

"Biel," Sam said, turning his vibro shield off and grabbing the private by the shoulders. He hauled him to his feet behind the corner of the building. "We need you right now. Let Doc do his job and you do yours. Do you understand me?"

Biel said nothing, his eyes wide and darting.

"Do you *understand* me?" Sam yelled, shaking Biel as hard as he could. "Get back in this fight! Use whatever it is that you're feeling right now and dust the sectoids that did this!"

"Oorah," Biel said quietly but firmly. He'd snapped out of whatever trance had overtaken him. "Oorah to that, Sarge."

Sam let him go.

"We're going to have to fall back," Captain Zeno said, peppering the approaching enemy from around the corner of the building. "Thompson, Jarman, get down here and take up Sergeant Samson's position until I give the order to leave. Doc, I want us moving as soon as you're finished up."

"Almost done," Doc said, slapping a skinpack where he'd pulled away Hall's armor and synthprene bodysuit. "I'll carry him."

The firing continued. The Iron Wolves were making the funneled horde of sectoids pay for every inch.

"We're in position!" Jarman called over the L-comm.

"Just in time," Zeno replied. "Iron Wolves, fall back! Use the buildings for cover. My element here will provide what suppressive fire we can."

Doc had Hall over his shoulders in a fireman's carry. "Ready when you are."

"Vibro shields!" Captain Zeno ordered.

Moon, Biel, and Sam joined the captain in forming a shield wall. They fired through it at the advancing enemy while Doc retreated with the wounded Hall.

The captain had cut this one close. Too close. The sectoids were practically on top of them, and upon seeing legionnaires finally in the open, they charged.

CHAPTER 28

"I'm out!" Moon shouted. He dropped his N-1 and pulled an arm-length machete from his side.

"Sola! Minh!" Captain Zeno yelled as the first wave of sectoids closed in on their shield wall. "We're falling back now. Kill box is all yours!"

The sectoids didn't waste blaster fire against the shields. Instead they ran forward, crashing against the legionnaires and using their naturally bladed forearms. It was a test of strength. Ancient combat like something out of a nightmare, but Sam's nightmares were worse than this. He could handle a swarm of red-faced bugs with clacking teeth.

Pound for pound, the legionnaires outmuscled their attackers, but each second saw another mercenary arrive to add their weight to the pressing attack. Captain Zeno and Biel blasted them at close range and picked off any that attempted to circle around them. The legionnaires backpedaled, doing everything they could to avoid being overrun.

Pain lanced up Sam's left arm, a dull soreness that came from holding the vibro shield in place. Although the shield itself weighed practically nothing, the constant battering against the barrier by the mercenary force was taking a toll.

The sectoids screamed their alien war cries.

Sam had an answer for them.

He pressed the blue button on the vambrace, activating the shield's razor-sharp edges. Then he pulled the thick war hammer from his back.

A sectoid charged at Sam, seeking to flank him. Sam thrust his shield up, and the blue energy blade cut through the mercenary's skull like a hot poker through a slab of butter.

The alien uttered an unsettling *Screee!* before Sam forced the shield through the rest of its skull, cutting it in half and dropping the sectoid to the street with the rest of its dead merc friends.

Another sectoid sought to take advantage of Sam's new shield positioning, but Sam crushed its skull with a mighty swing of his war hammer.

All was chaos and confusion. Everywhere Sam looked, he could see nothing but sectoids. They were pushing forward endlessly, impaling themselves on the vibro shields or dropping under the heavy blows of Sam's war hammer or the remaining blasts from the N-1s.

Moon shouted a frantic warning. "Biel! Watch—"

A grenade detonated just in front of Biel's shield. Whether it was dropped accidentally by one of his immediate attackers or thrown by some merc farther back who valued his own life more than his comrades, Sam didn't know. It didn't matter to Biel. He was thrown backward, his shield sputtering and then going dead. A gap of bleeding sectoids smoked where he'd last stood, but the gap was immediately filled by more advancing mercenaries seeking to take advantage of the situation.

Moon lost his footing and stumbled behind the captain.

That's it, Sam thought to himself.

"Sergeant!" Captain Zeno screamed into his comm. He threw his empty N-1 to the side and unsheathed the curved sword at his back. "Get these Wolves out of here! I'll hold them off you as long as I can."

Sam's mind was racing on overdrive. Surely they had made it back far enough for Minh and Sola to arrive and dust these kelhorned mercs, but they weren't here. All Sam could see was another hundred or more sectoids and their mounts spreading out to flank them on both sides, but the captain had given his orders.

Sam ran to Biel's side. The grenade must have exploded beneath the shield, because the legionnaire's legs were bleeding profusely. His body was still, no rise and fall of the chest. Sam's HUD showed Biel had life signs—but he was critical.

The leej was beyond hope. They'd come back for his body later.

Sam ran to see if Moon could walk on his own.

"You good?" he asked, skidding to a halt.

A sectoid streaked around their flank. Moon answered Sam's question by lurching to his feet, hacking his machete into the mercenary's neck, and ripping the blade down through its chest.

Captain Zeno backtracked toward them. Sam placed his back to Moon and the captain. He sliced a sectoid with his vibro shield and collapsed the skull of another with his war hammer.

Everything was going to hell. They were completely surrounded.

Where the heck are Sola and Minh? Sam gritted his teeth, rivulets of sweat running into his eyes. *At least Doc and Hall got away, and I'm not going down alone. I'm taking as many of these pieces of scum with me as I can.*

Sam took a blaster bolt in his left thigh. The armor did its job, but the force of the blast was enough to drop him to a knee.

A sectoid ran toward him, its bladed arm up and ready to bite into his bucket, when a flurry of blaster fire dropped the creature. More fire poured in, and the sectoids looked to their left and right in confusion, their charge broken.

"Sorry about the delay," came a voice over the comm. It was Minh. "We ran into a smaller sectoid force trying to flank you. We're here now."

"Light 'em up!" Captain Zeno yelled. "Keep givin' 'em hell!"

The din of war increased tenfold. Weapons fire exploded in the air all around Sam. Detonating grenades shook the ground beneath their feet.

"We're here too!" Sola's voice was like music to Sam's ears. Fenra howled in the background. "Same trouble. Sorry about the delay!"

The three legionnaires were still surrounded, but now the sectoids were looking outward rather than inward, chattering away in their native tongue, trying to assess the new threat. From every direction, red blaster fire was eating them alive. Sola, Colonel Minh, and their two hundred Conongan militiamen were using the kill box to devastating effect.

"Targets are in the kill basket and going down!" Minh screamed into the comms. "Heads down, Iron Wolves! Cononga fights with you! *Rah!*"

Sam had a hard time believing this take-charge leader was the same man he'd had to give a tongue-lashing to the day before.

"Fenra is coming over to clear you a way out," Sola yelled over the roar of weapons fire. "You'll know her when you see her. She'll be the massive bulldozer ripping her way toward you."

Sam shoved a sectoid back with his shield, broke its legs with the war hammer, then rammed the bladed shield down into the creature's chest. It bit deep through white armor and red flesh alike, slicing the merc in two.

Screaming, Sam hammered his shield down on the alien again and again. He knew the value of controlled rage, of unleashing the inner beast that lived just under the surface... but here he was losing it again. Lashing out at a combatant no longer in the fight, when danger remained.

A beep from his vambrace snapped him out of it. It was able to cut through the enemy with ease, but at a price. Its power readings were critically low. It couldn't keep this up.

To his left, Sam saw Fenra moving toward them. The lyconlore had strapped on a heavy chest piece, shielding her torso from enemy shots. She tore through the sectoids, ripping them apart with claws and teeth. Lifeless sectoid bodies became her shields as she waded into the chaos.

The tide had turned. The sectoids were now on the defensive, seeking a way out of the trap they'd fallen into, before none of them remained alive to tell the tale.

Fenra lifted a sectoid off the ground and twisted its neck so severely that its two black eyes were looking behind it. Then the lyconlore used the sectoid's body to absorb a burst of fire from the next mercenary she raged toward. She moved quickly, causing death and destruction, before skidding to a halt beside the legionnaires.

"Cavalry's here, let's go!" Captain Zeno thundered, sinking his shield into the head of one of the four-legged beasts of burden that had reached his position. The bug's entire black exoskeleton cranium crumpled with a gush of blood and gore. Its body quivered and shook in death spasms.

The three legionnaires followed behind the lyconlore. Most of the sectoids were now running in the opposite direction, and those that stayed to line up shots, or attempted to follow, were cut down by Minh's militia.

"Run, Wolves!" Minh shouted. "We'll cover you! Run!"

Green blood pooled in the streets. Sam had to be careful of his footing as he jumped over and sidestepped corpse after corpse.

After a few minutes of sprinting, Captain Zeno called a halt in the same town square in which they'd been welcomed as heroes when first arriving in the city. The palace was right behind them a few blocks to the south.

"Hold here," Captain Zeno said over the comms, sounding barely winded. "Iron Wolves report in."

For a moment static was the only reply, making Sam's stomach twist in his gut. Then Doc's voice came through.

"I got Hall stabilized and back to the palace," he said between heavy breaths. "I'm on your six now."

Sam looked behind him to see Doc sprinting from the palace to rejoin the unit.

Bean answered next. "Troy and I circled around. We're just a few minutes out from the rendezvous."

That was everyone accounted for except for Jarman and Thompson—and Sola reported on their status.

"I got your two boys with me," she said, sounding stressed and right in the thick of it. The legionnaires may have pulled back, but the Conongan militia was still in the fight. "They're in bad shape, but refusing to fall back. They both need to see your medic."

"Captain, we're fine!" Jarman shouted over the comm in his thick, barbaric accent. "We can stay and fight!"

"I'm sure you can handle it," Captain Zeno said with a hint of pride, "but there's still a lot of fighting left to be done, and I need you here. Fall back and let Dobson fix you up. You'll get more soon. I can promise you that."

"Roger that," Thompson and Jarman both said.

While the captain coordinated with the rest of his men, Sam turned his attention to Fenra. The lyconlore was splattered with blood. Her pupils were dilated, and her chest was heaving. She looked amped to the max. Sam wondered if his rages made him look something like that. Just smaller.

"You okay?" he asked, searching her for wounds. Not that he was much of a medic when it came to non-human injuries, but he knew enough to look for matted patches of red fur instead of green.

Fenra nodded and growled. Not menacingly, but neither did it mean anything to Sam.

He looked up at her and smiled. "You know I have no idea what you're saying, but man am I glad you're on our side. You feeling up to a quick weapons run? This shield and axe got me this far, but I need to get a blaster in my hands."

Fenra nodded.

Sam was just about to clear the idea with the captain and go searching for more weapons when Minh's elated voice filled the comms.

"We have the sectoids retreating! We've done it!"

"Well done," said Captain Zeno. "Now get your men—"

But Minh was immediately back on the comm, the jubilation in his voice replaced with a stunned horror. "No... How did they get here so fast?"

"Colonel Minh," Zeno said, stern as ever. "What's your status?"

"Rebel soldiers are entering the city. They have a—"

The colonel's voice was cut off by a deafening explosion that could be heard over comm... and everywhere else in the city.

CHAPTER 29

An entire building to Sam's right erupted into a ball of flames. Smoke mixed with dirt and debris billowed into the sky. Cononga's short night was coming to a close, and the shift in light was starting to play with his visor's optimized vision display.

He switched to a naked view, seeing through his bucket what he would see with his eyes unaided. The city was still wrapped in shadows, but the first rays of the morning sun crested over the tops of the trees and highest buildings.

"What was that thing?" Doc Dobson asked.

Sam knew right away. The rebels had somehow moved that massive piece of artillery with them, and evidently had it assembled and operational. His mind echoed Minh's question: How had they gotten it here so fast?

You should have destroyed it when you had the chance.

He shook the thought from his mind. The truth was, he had never really had that chance. In the enemy encampment, he'd lacked the tools, and the time, to do that sort of a job. Short of packing a kill team in his back pocket to slag the thing with an inferno charge, he'd done everything he could.

But his mind… sometimes it was his worst enemy. Whether it was losing control he ought to maintain, or beating him up for things legitimately beyond his control, it sometimes seemed to be fighting for the other side.

Troy and Bean appeared from the right and rejoined the group in the city square.

"Minh, come in!" Captain Zeno shouted into the comms. "Colonel Minh?"

Nothing.

"We've got company," Sola said. She sounded like she'd just picked herself up off the deck. "The rebels are entering the city, and they have a massive cannon mounted on the back of a gigantic repulsor truck. I'm pulling my forces back and spreading them out. I'm not going to give them a target."

"Understood," Captain Zeno said. "Can you see what happened to Colonel Minh and his men?"

"I can barely see anything in all this dust and debris," Sola said, coughing as she spoke.

"Roger. Get back to the square and we'll regroup."

Sola didn't bother answering.

Moon was full of energy, bouncing on the balls of his feet. "Sir, you don't need a weapons tech to tell you that we have to take that gun out ASAP if we're going to have a chance."

"Agreed," Zeno said. "That thing surely is good for more than one shot. Let's try to take it down as they reload. I don't imagine it's a quick process."

Sam stepped forward. "Captain, permission to take Moon, Bean, and Troy to gather up weapons for preparation to assault the cannon."

"Big old hammer not cutting it, Sergeant?"

Sam grinned behind his bucket. "As much as I'd like to cave in each and every one of their skulls with it, we need some ranged firepower."

"Go, but keep close enough to our lines that you don't get cut off," Zeno ordered. "Sola, I want last known enemy troop movements."

Sam motioned for Moon, Bean, and Troy to follow him while they listened to Sola's report over the comm.

"We put more than a dent into the sectoids that entered the kill box," Sola answered. "I'd say, at a minimum, sixty percent casualties from their ranks. What survived linked up with the rebel force just entering the city."

Sam clicked his comm to a channel reserved for only nearby Iron Wolves. "Moon, Bean, Troy, keep your heads down. We're here to collect weapons and ammunition only."

Three voices returned Sam's order. "Roger."

Sam crouched low, shield off and the war hammer slung across his back. The street ahead of them was full of smoke and debris—some of it from the fighting, most of it from the building the rebel cannon had razed. Moans from dying sectoids filled the air like ghosts coming back from the dead to haunt those that had sent them to their graves.

Sectoid bodies filled the street where the Conongans had sprung their attack—and bodies meant weapons. It wouldn't take long to get everyone stocked up with new blasters.

"Careful, these mercs might be playing dead, ready to shoot us when we get close," Bean warned, leaning down to grab a sectoid blaster pistol with his good arm.

There was a variety of weapons, but the preferred blaster was a long black rifle known as an Anvil P9. It packed enough recoil that most humanoids wouldn't shoot one unless they were armored.

Sam grabbed two from a pair of dead mercs. He was sure they were dead—one was ripped open from groin to chest, the other was missing a section of its head. He squatted down to check the corpses for additional charge packs.

"Hey, we got a live one here," Moon said. He was standing over a sectoid that was gurgling green blood, struggling to breathe. "Kind of want to leave him alive and make him suffer as long as possible."

Sam found himself caught in an internal debate he'd had numerous times on the battlefield. KTF left no room for mercy, but as he listened to the labored breathing of the dying sectoid, he couldn't help himself. He pulled a blade from the dead merc he'd just stripped of ammunition, and walked over to the alien clinging to the last tendrils of life.

You're wrong for doing this, Sam.

His mind remained ever against him.

"Sarge, don't do it," Bean spat. "Let him live and suffer. I heard what happened to Biel."

"Shut up, Bean." Sam drove the blade through the sectoid's right eye, deep into the cavern of its alien skull.

The other three legionnaires watched silently as Sam pulled the blade back out and dropped it, dripping with gore, onto the creature's lifeless torso.

No words needed to be spoken.

"I, uh... I found some grenades and a crate of charge packs on one of those big bugs they were riding," Troy said. His tone was light, as if he had told a joke, even though he hadn't. When you were a legionnaire you laughed things off, or you let them eat you up inside. Sometimes both. "I should probably carry it. Bean wouldn't be able to lift it with both his scrawny arms, let alone one."

"You checking out my arms again?" Bean asked. "Listen, if you need to talk about your feelings for me, I want you to know I accept you as you are."

"Please," Troy said with a laugh. "Only thing you'll be accepting is my foot up your ass."

There was the laughter, but while the banter might be good for the men, sending jabs back and forth over squad comm wasn't going to keep their heads in the game. "Stow the chatter, you two," Sam said. "Focus on getting what we need and getting back. I'm gonna look for Biel. We should take him back while we have the chance."

The mention of Biel brought the men's levity to an end rather more abruptly than Sam had intended.

He had walked a few yards up the street, and was stooping to remove a grenade belt and another Anvil P9, when he spotted someone moving down the street in their direction.

"Movement, twelve o'clock."

He raised one of the heavy P9s and pressed himself against a doorframe on the building to his left. Immediately the other legionnaires dropped to their knees or stomachs to take up fire positions.

"Easy, Legionnaires!" shouted the figure walking toward them. He held his hands up, palms forward. "I just want to talk."

It was the green aline commander. The scum sack who had beaten Sola. He had to know that approaching legionnaires like this was a surefire way to get himself killed.

"Want me to dust him?" Moon asked over comms from his position on the other side of the street. "Give me the word, Sarge, and he's in the ground."

Something about the brazen way the commander approached made Sam pause. Maybe whatever he had to say was something Captain Zeno needed to hear.

"No. Don't fire."

"Legionnaires!" The rebel commander's voice echoed among the dead as he continued walking forward. "My world-eater is loaded and aimed at the palace as we speak. Did you not see what it did to its previous target? Did you not witness it crumble to the ground? The palace could be destroyed with only a word. But… such is not my wish."

"He serious, Sarge?" Bean asked.

Sam didn't know, but it didn't seem like a chance he could take.

"Noi is mine, as is all of Cononga, but what good is conquering a nation if you destroy everything in the process? I suggest you hear what I have to say."

"Hold your fire," Sam reminded his team on L-comm, though there was little more that he wanted right now than to dust the green-skinned rebel. On external speaker he addressed the alien. "Stay where you are. There's no ruling a nation if you're dead."

"You won't kill me, Legionnaire," the commander said confidently. "And I intended already to go no further."

Sam called Zeno directly over L-comm. "Captain, we have the rebel leader here saying he has that cannon trained on the palace. Says he wants to talk. Should we dust him?"

"No. Do not engage. I'm on my way." Captain Zeno's voice came quick and hard as if he were already running to their position. "I'll be there in a few minutes."

Sam spoke once more to the alien. "Our commander is en route."

The rebel leader nodded. "Very well."

Sam didn't lower his weapon, keeping the rebel lined up in his crosshairs. His finger itched to squeeze the trigger. But ending the alien's life would likely result in mission failure, and without the palace to fall back to, his men would be overrun and hunted down one by one inside the city.

As Sam waited for the captain to arrive, his gaze drifted down the street. There, just two hundred yards behind the rebel commander, lay the body of Biel. Sam's brother. Lying amid the carnage of slain mercenaries, his body already cooling.

For a moment he imagined he saw the legionnaire sit up and point accusingly at the rebel commander responsible for his death. Sam knew what Biel—the ghost of Biel—wanted. *Kill him.*

Sam shook off the hallucination. He needed rest. Things… things were catching up to him.

Still, he slid his finger inside the P9's guard and rested it against the trigger.

Don't do it, he told himself. *You heard the captain. He gave you a direct order. What are you thinking?*

Sam knew exactly what he was thinking. It involved a blaster bolt ripping through the smug alien commander's eyes.

Captain Zeno's arrival came as a relief.

The captain's voice came hushed over the comms. "Use this time to gather as many weapons and supplies as you can."

The legionnaires went to work. All except for Sam, who stayed fixed in his position, not taking his eyes off the rebel. The aline was wearing thick body armor, but no helmet, revealing that self-assured, unbearable smile of his. The smile of a man who knows he's won.

"I'm Captain Zeno. What is it you wanted to say?" The captain stopped at Sam's side, an Anvil P9 of his own in his hands. "If you've come to surrender," he continued, "the terms are unconditional."

This seemed to amuse the alien. His smile grew even more smug, if that were possible. "We haven't even been properly introduced. We're hardly at a point where we can begin speaking about terms of surrender." The rebel commander stepped closer. The three slashes across his face, courtesy of Fenra, were now scars—he'd likely been treated by skinpacks. "My name is Commander Tor."

Sam pressed his own Anvil P9 closer to his shoulder. On external speakers, he said, "Permission to kill him now, Captain?"

For the first time, something other than superiority flashed across the enemy commander's eyes. It was there for only a second, but the look was unmistakable. *Fear.*

"You would be wise to *control* your soldiers," Tor said.

"Lower your weapon, Sergeant," Captain Zeno said, also over external speaker. He added over L-comm, "Though there's nothing I'd like more than for you to dust the kelhorn."

"Yes, sir." Sam lowered his weapon.

"Very good," Commander Tor said. "Though that little show suggests that you legionnaires are not realizing how hopeless your cause is. Nor how serious *I* am. Perhaps a demonstration is in order."

Before either legionnaire could object, Commander Tor lifted his right arm into the air with a closed fist.

The ground shook as if the commander had somehow started his own earthquake.

CHAPTER 30

Behind the aline appeared the massive barrel of the great cannon, roaring into view at the outskirts of the city. It was pointed upward, as though it planned to shatter the heavens. Even without the earlier demonstration, its appearance left no doubt that this was a weapon capable of destroying an entire building with one shot.

"What you are seeing is our super cannon, our *world-eater*." Commander Tor's smug smile appeared once more on his green face. The skin flaps that dangled over his upper lip twitched as he grinned. "While on the repulsor truck, it's capable of taking down entire buildings, as you have seen. Once offloaded onto solid ground, it will be able to shoot down vehicles in low orbit, like, say... *Republic transports*."

Sam's gut tightened. He had no love for Major Roy somewhere high overhead in the *Breaker*, but there were hundreds of crewmembers up there he *did* care about. Friends. Brothers. Fellow Iron Wolves. If Tor wasn't lying... the stakes just got a lot higher.

"So which is it?" Zeno asked. "Palace or transport? Because you only get one shot before I drop you."

"Oh, I never had any intention of destroying the palace," Tor practically purred. "It's my future home. That was simply bait to draw you out, Captain."

Captain Zeno nodded appreciatively. "In that case..."

In a flash, his rifle was at his shoulder and a scoring blaster bolt was screaming at Tor's head. It passed right through the commander's skull and struck a building further up the street.

The captain had just scored a headshot on a hologram.

"I'm disappointed in you, Captain," said Tor. "You do me a disservice thinking I would expose myself in such a way. Like the world-eater, I am safely beyond your reach, I assure you."

"Either way, you're done here. I've already transmitted a warning to any Republic ships in orbit. You have no targets left."

"Done?" Commander Tor threw back his holographic head and laughed. "Not at all. The palace will be spared. As for all those remaining in the city... that is another matter, or did you think the device you captured was our *only* biological weapon?"

Sam gritted his teeth. This was going from bad to worse.

Evidently Zeno felt the same way. "So what is it you want, Tor? You want us to roll over and die?"

"My demands are much simpler than that, Captain. Just go home." Tor stated his condition as though it was the easiest thing to do in the universe, and in a way... it was.

"Go home, Legionnaires. Leave us. Leave Cononga. The majority of us are not like Cononga. We don't want you or your Republic here. This isn't your fight. This isn't your *planet*. Go back to your families. Just go."

"And what?" Sam asked, shaking his head. "Leave you to rule? Leave you to install a dictatorship over these people?"

"You miss my point," Commander Tor sneered. "*Whatever* I choose to do, it's no concern of yours. Do I tell you who should rule your galaxy? Or how? Do I make demands of your House of Reason or your Senate? Leave now, Legionnaires. My offer will not stand forever."

"Suppose we refuse your generous offer?" Captain Zeno asked.

"Then I will poison this city, depriving you of your remaining Conongan allies. When you cry to the Republic for help, I will have my world-eater pluck the first shuttle or transport from the sky. No one will save you as I march my army through the center of this town."

"You're wrong," Sam said, once again speaking without thinking. "You do that, and you start a war with the Republic, and the first destroyer that shows up will turn everything around you—including that big gun—to atoms."

Tor shook his head, a disdainful lopsided grin on his face. "Sergeant, I deal in reality, not fantasy. You expect me to believe that the Republic cares about so small a force as yourself? That they will start a war because a few legionnaires died somewhere at galaxy's edge? If they cared, you and your fellow legionnaires would not be in this position. They don't, and you know it. You know it better than anyone."

Sam swallowed hard. He didn't *know* it, but there had been plenty of times when he had *thought* it. More times than he cared to count.

Yet... did it matter? Did it matter whether the Republic had his back? Was he doing it for them? Was that why he was here, fighting for a people he'd met only days ago, on a backwater planet far from anywhere he'd ever called home?

No. It's not. It's not now, and it never was.

Sergeant Sam Samson wasn't fighting for the Senate, or the House, or even the Republic. He was fighting for the Legion. For his brothers. For Zeno. For Biel.

For PFC Allen Valdez.

The Republic didn't even want him in this fight in the first place, but it was the right thing to do.

"What do you think, Sergeant Samson?" Captain Zeno asked. "Shall the Wolves turn tail and run?"

Sam cocked his head to the side as if giving it some thought. "That's a good question, Captain Zeno. I'm glad you asked." He stroked his chin. "I have to say, Commander Tor is making a lot of sense to me right now."

A devilish grin blossomed on Tor's face.

"The thing is..." Sam continued, "I like the weather here. The people, too. Other than those rebel kelhorns. You know, Captain... I think we'd better stay."

Sam pointed a finger at the commander's hologram and his voice changed from pleasant to cold. "But *you*. I'll be looking for you on the battlefield. I'll be the last thing you see. You can believe that."

The grin on Tor's face disappeared. His eyes bulged out of his head. As he spoke, spittle found its way from his mouth and past the overhanging flesh that fell from his upper lip. "I will kill every single one of you!" he screamed. "There will be nothing left!"

"That's enough talking," Captain Zeno said calmly, lifting his weapon. "You want this city? *Come and take it*, and don't think we're not ready for what you're threatening."

"Fools! You insolent, stubborn fools!" Commander Tor screamed. "I will see you dead if it—"

The hologram was extinguished with a trigger pull from Captain Zeno.

Zeno shrugged. "I spotted the bot that was rendering him."

Sam looked over at his captain. "You think he really has another one of those bio-weapons?"

"Can't say, but any choice except fighting meant a death sentence for these people, besides, I never planned on living forever."

Sam nodded. "Orders?"

"He'll regroup and come at us fast. Commander Tor doesn't strike me as the patient type. We'll retreat back to the palace. It's the most defensible position."

"Roger that," Sam said. "Wolves, as riveting as that was, I'd better see you loaded down with weapons."

"Even fashioned a stretcher to carry them," Moon said.

"I got a better use for the stretcher," Zeno said. He walked down the street to Biel's body. "Let's get our brother on there. We'll carry our gear back to the palace."

Sam squatted down next to Biel. "Sir, I can get him. Stock up the stretcher with charge packs. Please. Let me carry him."

Zeno nodded in understanding. "All right, Leej. You do that."

Sam swallowed hard, pushing down his emotions. He knew they needed venting, for the sake of his own sanity, but that would have to come later. For now, he hoisted Biel's lifeless body over his shoulders. In his leej armor, the dead man was heavy, but Sam would still have carried his brother even if he weighed another hundred pounds.

Captain Zeno placed a hand on Biel's body. "Your fight's over now." He looked to the other legionnaires. "He didn't forget nothin'."

Sam and the rest of the Iron Wolf expedition party slipped inside the Conongan defensive line and jogged to the palace courtyard. Sola was waiting for them there, armed now with her own Anvil T9. She looked as though she was going to say something, then clammed up as the legionnaires approached.

"Speak up," Captain Zeno said to her, motioning for her to join them as they continued to move. "Colonel Minh and the president trusted you enough to put you in charge of a detachment of the militia, so that makes you a national leader—small as this country might be. Go ahead and act like it."

Sola nodded. "Yes, sir. I have the rest of the men setting up around the palace." She motioned to the structure in the distance. "The wounded are being cared for there as well. We've scavenged enough weapons and armor from the sectoids for another stand. Honestly, we're better equipped now than ever."

"How many of the militia can you account for?" Zeno asked.

"That building they took out... Minh was there, along with most of his force. His men that have rejoined us report heavy casualties from the explosion. Minh was among the dead." Sola shook her head sorrowfully. "All told, only eighty Conongan militia have returned to the palace. So far."

"Plus the Iron Wolves—and one lyconlore," Sam said. He looked over at Fenra to see how she liked his comment. She just shrugged with her tongue lolling out of the side of her mouth.

"We can hold," Captain Zeno said. "First priority is to take care of that cannon. If by some miracle the Republic comes to its senses and decides to give us a hand, we want the drop shuttles to be able to get down here in one piece."

"There should be enough explosives in the armory to get the job done," Sam said. Between the det-brick and all the grenades and fraggers they'd collected, they could build themselves a nice bomb.

"Good." Zeno looked around. "Where's my weapons tech?"

"Here, sir." Private Moon came running up.

"You heard the rebel commander. Let's assume for the moment he's telling the truth about having another bio-weapon. How can we neutralize it?"

"Well, sir, that's a really open-ended scenario. We don't know if it's even the same weapon, but if it's like the other weapon we found, the chemical is stable in its liquid form. If we can figure out where they're setting it up, maybe we can steal it before they can use it?"

"Roger that." Captain Zeno turned to the rest of the squad. "Change of plans, Wolves. This palace remains the last stand—for the Conongan militia, but we leejes have other work to do. We're going hunting."

CHAPTER 31

The palace courtyard was a maelstrom of activity, and the steps leading up to the palace were a maze of sandbags and razor wire. The Conongan militia had turned the area into a battlefield. They gave the Iron Wolves grim nods of admiration as they passed, but when Sam passed by them carrying Biel's body, each man stood at attention with a hand raised in salute. Soon, every Conongan soldier was standing to offer what respect they could to the fallen Iron Wolf.

Lyn and President Gen came out of the palace dressed in white aprons and gloves, splattered with blood. It seemed they had found a way to help despite their lack of military training.

Sam gently handed over Biel's body to one of the medical orderlies buzzing around the president and Senate liaison. The orderlies respectfully took the body off toward the casualty collection point.

A shouting sounded from the palace steps. "Here they come!"

The Conongan soldier was only half right. Tor had led his rebel army and the remains of the sectoid force through the largely undefended city, but he now brought them to a halt on the far side of the town square, well beyond the effective fire of the P9s both armies were now equipped with. It would be near impossible to get off an accurate shot at this distance unless someone had a high-powered sniper rifle.

Behind them hummed the massive repulsor truck carrying the cannon. It looked even larger now that it was assembled—like an impervisteel silo. Its barrel could not only hold Sam, but Fenra—and she could stretch out comfortably.

The repulsor truck began to adjust its mount to lower the weapon to the ground.

"They're going to make us watch them shoot the *Breaker* out of the sky," Sam said.

Zeno shook his head. "Well, they'll be disappointed then. I sent an all-comm warning for all Republic craft to leave orbit."

"Oh," said Lyn. "Oh, dear."

"What?" asked Sam, almost afraid to ask.

"The major *did* receive your message, Captain, but... he didn't believe it."

"What?"

"He contacted me. I didn't know what to say—I didn't want to let him know what you all were doing. I got the impression he thinks we're making it up in an attempt to authorize strikes against the rebels. As far as I know, he's, uh... he's still in orbit."

"We have to tell him again," Sam said.

"We do that and he'll just dig in his heels deeper," Captain Zeno said, shaking his head. "If there's one thing I know about points, they'll go to any lengths to avoid admitting they've made a mistake. Sket. I've got men up there!"

"Sir, we have to try," insisted Sam. "We should at least do that much."

"Moon." Zeno turned to the private. "How long do you think we have before they can get a shot off against the *Breaker*?"

Moon considered the behemoth in the distance. "They'll probably have to do some plasma digging to get it anchored properly. At least, if you're going for optimal operations to reach a target in orbit like that. If I were them, I'd—"

"*Moon*—how long?" Sam said, interrupting.

"Two hours at the very soonest," Moon said, nodding his head along with his assessment.

Thompson and Jarman appeared from inside the palace. The former was limping while the latter's right arm was in a sling.

Troy teased them. "Well, lookee here. Thought we'd never see you poor excuses for leejes again."

Thompson threw a thumb over his shoulder. "Doc didn't exactly clear us, but he can't stop us either."

"Glad to have you back in action," the captain said. "Now, everyone, listen up. Sergeant Samson and I will contact the *Breaker* to tell them of the danger—again—though I'm not expecting much. You men make sure you're kitted out with the best of what we have available. It'll be up to us to take down that weapon and save our people in orbit. I'll organize a diversion with the militia."

"Roger," a chorus of voices answered back.

The unit dispersed, leaving Sam and the captain alone. Both men flipped their comms over to the channel shared with the *Breaker*.

"*Breaker*, this is Captain Zeno for Major Roy."

A tech's voice came over the comms. "Captain Zeno, this is the *Breaker*. Hold for Major Roy."

"Understood."

A moment later Major Roy's distinct voice came over the channel. "Captain Zeno. Nice of you to finally answer my requests for status. Have things come to an end? Has the conflict been resolved?"

"That would be a negative, sir." Captain Zeno forged ahead without giving the major a chance to respond to that. "But we have definitive intel that the rebels attacking the Conongans have a super cannon capable of reaching the *Breaker* in no more than two hours. I have been informed by the rebel commander, an aline named Tor, that they intend to use it for just that purpose. Please be advised to leave orbit."

"A super cannon?" Major Roy repeated the words like he had never heard the two used together before. "Captain, your sources must be incorrect. Our reports show the inhabitants of this planet are incapable of that level of technology."

"Sir..." Captain Zeno leaned back to look out the palace gates, across the square, and at the cannon in the far distance, "I'm looking at it *now*. Transmitting visuals. I've seen it take down a building, and I do believe it will be able to reach the *Breaker*."

"You saw it take down a building?" Major Roy bristled, and his voice grew heated. "Captain, I'm seeing your visuals. That thing is big, but it's hardly high-tech. It looks like it's more likely to blow up the rebels than get a shot into orbit. More to the point, Captain Zeno, you and the Iron Wolves were *ordered* to sit this one out until the conflict subsided. You were *further* ordered to return to the *Breaker* should the situation escalate. I'd say entire buildings being destroyed constitutes an escalation of the situation, Captain!"

"Sir, we were caught in the middle of a war." Captain Zeno was as cool and calm as ever. "A war in which one side is looking to slaughter and enslave the other. We're legionnaires. We can't sit these kinds of things out. My men are—"

"Your men," Roy snapped, "are following a commander who will be *court-martialed* if he doesn't *immediately* await extraction at the airfield—"

"My men are keeping innocent blood from being spilled!" Zeno shouted, finally losing his cool.

There was a tense silence over the comm before Major Roy spoke again. His voice was as icy as Sam had ever heard it. "Captain, you and your men are ordered back to the *Breaker* immediately. You will be placed under arrest upon arrival and will remain so until you face a tribunal to account for your direct disobedience of—"

Captain Zeno disconnected the feed.

He removed his helmet and ran a dirty hand through his short black hair. His face was grimy—even his eye patch was smeared with a mixture of sweat and dirt. He retrieved his canteen, unscrewed the lid with trembling hands, and took a long swig. Then he poured water over his head as Sam stood by in silence.

Sam had never seen the captain so rattled.

"What do you think, Sergeant?" Zeno asked finally. "Backs against the wall at the edge of the universe. Enemy's going to force us to attack them, outnumbered five to one, and if we survive, I've got a future in the synth mines waiting for me."

"That won't happen, sir. Once Legion Command hears the *reason* for your doing this... no way you go to Herbeer." Sam looked out at the looming cannon. Plasma drills were already hard at work digging down to secure the massive weapon. "Call me crazy, but even outnumbered—even if I knew this meant a prison sentence—I'd stand and fight this battle every time. I'm right where I'm supposed to be, sir, and so are you."

"Glad to hear I'm not the only one who's crazy." Captain Zeno screwed the top on his canteen. "But that's what makes you a great legionnaire. You just have to learn to control the crazy a little better when things get intense. Do that for me, will you, Sam?"

Sam looked down.

"Okay," Zeno said, not pressing the issue. "I'm going to take Moon, Troy, and Bean out the back of the palace and see if we can't get eyes on this bio-weapon. That cannon is yours. Gotta divide and conquer, and I don't trust myself not to let the thing blow Roy out of orbit just to prove him wrong."

Sam nodded. It was all so stupid. All the Republic had to do was give them the smallest bit of support. A single bomber or starship would be the difference between total victory and ending up in a coffin. Just one ship. Anything would do. Any old—

Wait.

Sam blinked a few times as a plan came together. "Sir... I'm thinking we should head back to the airfield."

Zeno looked crestfallen.

"No, not like that. Troy's always going on about how back home he flies his little single-engine craft, right? The one he says he broke that flight record for and we laugh at him and call him a liar, but he insists he did? Well, I'm sure you noticed there was a ship in the hangar when we landed..."

Captain Zeno's eyes widened. "*That* thing? Sergeant, that ship was ancient if it was a day. Who knows when's the last time it even left the ground? Or if it ever will again."

"There's only one way to find out."

"I like it as a Plan B," Captain Zeno said firmly. "But for now, we stay on point and do what we can with what we know we have."

"Oorah, Captain. Let's give these kelhorns a fight to remember."

CHAPTER 32

"You're an idiot," Sola said, shaking her head. "I just want it to go on record that I tried to be the voice of reason here." She crossed her arms over her chest piece.

Sam shrugged. "I didn't say it was a *good* plan."

"It's the *worst* plan, Sam. You want to charge that cannon behind nothing but vibro shields!"

"Because it's what we've got, and all we have to do is get close enough to attach our Savage Wars explosive cocktail to one of the weapon's supports."

Sola scoffed. "Oh, is that 'all we have to do'? And all that stands in our way is two hundred yards of open ground and hundreds of rebel soldiers." She peered deep into Sam's eyes as if she were truly trying to understand him. "Seriously, where do they find you guys? I thought legionnaires were supposed to be battlefield geniuses. Tactical wizards. Do you have brain damage?"

"I *have* had a lot of concussions." Sam grinned. "So yeah, probably."

Sola rolled her eyes.

Sam looked out across the city. The sun was casting long morning shadows, but rolling clouds in the distance looked dark and angry, promising rain. All around the palace entrance, the Conongan soldiers were spread out, ready to fend off the overwhelming force that lingered in plain sight, out of range and unwilling to start the action before they had the opportunity to shoot down a Republic transport. Sam had to admit, this militia, though halved in number, was a far cry from the force that had just barely fought off the first rebel strike. They were now armed with T9s, grenades, and even a few Mullers—heavier weapons they'd taken from the sectoids. If they got overrun, it wouldn't be because they weren't prepared.

"Fenra wants to go with you," Sola said.

The lyconlore was nearby, piecing together white body armor sections taken from dead sectoids. It was a bloody business, tearing the exoskeleton from the mercenaries. She looked like an overgrown puppy tearing at chew toys—but much more gruesome.

"And what did you tell her?" Sam asked.

"That she's an idiot, just like you." Sola crossed her arms. "And... just like me."

"Like you?"

"Oh, don't think that means I'm going with you. I'm not *that* much of an idiot. I'm only insane enough to fight a losing battle for ideals, or morals, or whatever makes us stand here defending these people." Sola said the words in a rush, then paused. "I don't know if there's any hope of winning this thing."

"There's always hope," Sam said, looking deep into her eyes. "As long as we draw breath—and even when we don't, as long as others believe—then hope remains."

Sola laughed. "You missed your calling. You should have been a motivational speaker."

Sam grinned and looked once more past their defenses to the enemy encampment. Hundreds of rebels were working like tiny ants, preparing the cannon for use. He put on his helmet and used his visor to zoom in. Many of the rebels looked underfed and not of a strong fighting spirit. Hardly legionnaires, but in large enough numbers, they were a threat. And they certainly had the numbers.

"Sergeant, come in." Captain Zeno's voice came over the comms so low it immediately sent Sam into high alert.

"I'm here, Captain."

"We have eyes on the biological weapon. They set it up in a building parallel to the super cannon. Look a block to the east. There's a single-story building with a tan dome."

Sam fixed his sights on the cannon and panned to the east. While most of the rebels were working on the so-called world-eater, a large detachment—perhaps a hundred—was milling about the tan-domed building.

"What do you need me to do?" he asked. He was ready to give his life if the captain asked for it.

"I need you to create a distraction. Something big enough to give us a chance to storm the building by surprise."

"How much time do you need?"

Private Moon chimed in. "Shouldn't be long once we're inside, Sarge. All we need to do is remove the liquid vial from the machine. It's not harmful until it's been aerosolized."

"I'm with you," Sam said.

"Roger that," Captain Zeno said. "We'll wait for your signal."

"You'll know it when you see it, sir. Samson out."

Sam looked over to Sola, who was eyeing him expectantly. "You blanked out there for a while. On the Legion comm?"

"Yeah." He took a deep breath. "We're making the charge now."

Sola looked like she wanted to punch Sam's lights out. "I can't believe you're actually doing this."

"Has to be done, though."

Activating L-comm, Sam called for his team of legionnaires. "Doc, Thompson, Jarman. I need you all to report to my location." He pinged his position over HUD so the legionnaires could easily find him in the courtyard. "Our timetable has been pushed up. Captain needs a distraction, so we're making the assault on the super cannon now. Kill two spiders with one stomp."

"Roger that," answered Jarman. "I'm ready to KTF, but—point of order—you meant to say 'cats,' not 'spiders.' Kill two cats with one stomp."

"Really?" asked Thompson. "That's kinda nasty."

"That's how I remember the saying at least."

"Could be," Sam said, appreciating the levity of the moment. "But I hate spiders, so we're rolling with that. Jarman and Thompson, I need to know for sure if you're good to go."

"They're not," Doc said, his sober voice cutting into the comm chatter. "But it is what it is."

"I'll make it," Thompson said. Sam saw the legionnaire limping into view. "Let's do this."

Fenra appeared as well, as if sensing her time had come. The lyconlore had torn apart enough sectoids to make her own crude suit modeled after the Iron Wolves, using some kind of adhesive to patch it all together around her massive frame. She hadn't done a bad job.

Sam addressed her directly. "Fenra, there's been a change of plans. You're going to be central to this operation."

Sola groaned, but Fenra gave a wicked grin.

"There's going to be a ton of firepower coming at us, so I'm putting all of us leejes on vibro shield duty—covering *you*. Your job is to lob grenades over the shields and clear us a path to the super cannon. Think you can handle that?"

Fenra growled, low and menacing.

"I'll take that as a yes. Sola." Sam turned to the woman who'd started off as a guide and ended up as a pivotal leader of the Conongan defenses. "We're going all-in here. I want you to tell the militia to push as well. The shields should provide some clear lanes until they run out of juice."

Sola hissed and crossed her arms. "Fine," she said. "But we're all going to die because of this."

Doc and Thompson arrived at Sam's side. "No sign of Jarman yet?"

"Jarhead!" Sam called. "Where you at?"

"Armory, sir. I figure we don't want to forget that satchel of explosives we rigged together."

"Oorah, leej. You didn't forget nothin'."

Fenra snarled something.

"She wants to know what you think of her armor," Sola said.

"You look ready to KTF, Fenra," said Sam.

Fenra responded with one of her frightening smiles, then growled a deep-throated question at Sola.

"No, you're not joining the Legion after this," Sola answered, with playful derision. She turned to Sam. "She's excited for action. Like an idiot. Come to think of it, she really does have the brains to be a legionnaire."

"And the personal hygiene." Sam grinned. "Let's get going. I can see Jarman jogging up this way."

They trotted together to the inner courtyard. Sam waved his hand to his motley unit: Sola, Fenra, Doc, Thompson, and Jarman.

"Gear up!" he shouted. "We're about to do something crazy!"

CHAPTER 33

"You know if a blaster hits any of this, we're toast," Jarman said, kneeling with the others as they molded bits of plastic det-brick around grenades, increasing their explosive power. "Like... crater in the ground dead. So dead we'll make other people that are dead look alive. So dead that—"

"I get it," Sam said. He gathered the bomblets the legionnaires had assembled and put them in an armored pack used to carry high explosives in combat. If a rebel or sectoid did get a shot on target, hopefully the pack would be tough enough to withstand the blow. If not... well, they wouldn't have to worry about much after that.

In all, there were a dozen of the extra-strength bomblet grenades, each as large as one of Fenra's massive paws, and that didn't include the big daddy intended to take out the super cannon. That filled up another bag all on its own.

"We hold the shield line no matter what," Sam said, looking at Doc, Thompson, and Jarman, who all nodded back. "Our strength is that there's no weak link. We move forward, vibro shields up, no matter what. Keep Fenra covered. Between her tossing explosives and Sola making her push with the rest of the Conongan militia, we have a chance. Oorah?"

"Oorah!" the legionnaires shouted.

Fenra lifted her head to the darkening sky and let out a long piercing cry that sent a chill down Sam's spine.

"Captain, get ready," Sam said over comms as he took a position at the head of the stairs and activated his vibro shield. "We're going to get one chance at this."

"We're in position, Samson," Captain Zeno replied. "KTF for the win."

Four blue shields hummed with energy. They sizzled and sparked when they touched one another, but if the legionnaires were going to protect Fenra, they were going to need to make sure there was no gap in their wall. Thompson was on Sam's left, Doc on his right, and Jarman on the other side of Doc.

They placed their Anvil P9s in the square slots in their shields, ready to dish out damage as they advanced. All except Jarman—his wound wouldn't allow him to wield both the shield and an Anvil, so he'd be entirely focused on shielding their right flank.

As one they moved down the steps. Fenra followed low on all fours, making sure not a hair was exposed.

"Match my speed," Sam said. "We'll take them by surprise at first, but that edge will die quickly."

His heart was pounding in his chest with the promise of insanity at any moment. He felt the weight of the war hammer still on his back. It seemed so heavy all of a sudden. He wanted to shrug it off.

But what if you need it?

The four legionnaires and the lone lyconlore pressed forward to Sola, who was moving her troops to the forward line of defensive structures. She gave Sam a grim nod.

"We've got your back, Legionnaire. Move fast. I'm going to be pissed if you die."

"That makes two of us." Sam wished he had thought of something cooler to say. He picked up his speed, sending the legionnaires into a slow trot. Thompson's limp was noticeable, but he kept pace.

A shout went up from the rebel lines. They had spotted the four shining vibro shields and the soldiers behind them making their move. Then came the sounds of weapons being discharged. They were firing much too soon, but that was to be expected with a poorly trained opponent.

More concerning was the rebel foot soldiers who charged. The vibro shields would stop incoming fire, but with only four shields, the leejes could easily be flanked. They needed to move fast, aggressive—skewer the opponent before they knew what had hit them, and count on Sola to keep the enemy at bay.

Sam opened up with controlled bursts from his Anvil P9. Behind him and on both sides, the Conongan militia began to spray the enemy lines with blaster fire. The Conongans, too, could have used more training—precision aiming wasn't possible from their current distance. *Move them forward, Sola.*

Rebel blaster rounds began to strike the shields in high volume as the leejes moved within range. Sam felt the pressure build on his vambrace arm. There were so many rounds striking his shield at once that whatever technology the shield used to soften the blows was overloading. The charge pack was already beeping and at half strength. That didn't bode well.

Sam pressed forward. It was hard to even see anything past the blaster fire splashing across the shield.

If the vibro shield runs out of juice... what a way to go. We'll be eaten up like meat through a grinder.

"Come on, we can do this!" Sam shouted into the comms. In the face of this firepower, their steady trot now felt like an uphill march. "Stay together!"

"Oorah!" Doc shouted, leaning low. "We got this!"

Thompson and Jarman merely grunted in response. They were too focused on staying in position and moving forward to hold a conversation.

The only part of Sam that wasn't protected was his Anvil, poking through the hole in the shield. Against this volume of fire, it was inevitable it would be struck—and it was, by several shots at once. He was lucky to still have his fingers. He dropped the weapon and glanced over to the other legionnaires. The same fate had befallen them.

"Sola!" Sam shouted into the comm. "We could *really* use some supporting fire right about now."

"So could we!"

"Sket!" Sam pressed forward. Each step was a struggle. It felt like weightlifters were pushing them back from the other side, and he was seriously rethinking the wisdom of this crazy plan. If their shields were destroyed before they even got close enough for Fenra to begin lobbing those bombs—their great equalizer—they'd be dead before they'd even made a dent.

"Fenra!" Sam shouted. "How strong is that hairy arm of yours? Can you light 'em up from here?"

A roar emanated from behind him, and immediately something sailed over the shields—and with some serious air. It just reached the center of the rebel's gathered front line, which stretched along the top of the square, and one-hopped underneath a troop transport.

The explosion sent the vehicle flipping over in a ball of flame, flinging broken rebel bodies through the sky. A smoking crater at least twenty feet in diameter tore a terrific hole out of the rebel line.

"What the heck was that thing made of?" Thompson said, breathing hard. "Death?"

"I don't know," said Jarman, "but we could use a lot more of that. My shield is just about toast."

The chaos from the blast gave them a brief respite. It seemed that nearly every rebel had dropped to the ground, or was distracted by the massive blast. This was the leejes' chance to cover some ground. The lyconlore had a hell of an arm, but if she was to have a chance of hitting the super cannon with the big bomb, they would have to push for all they were worth.

"Let's go!" Sam said. "Give it all you got!"

The rebels quickly restarted their barrage, but now Fenra was well within her range, and was hurling explosive after explosive into the rebel ranks. The enemy lines devolved into a chaotic mess as the poorly trained troops scattered to avoid the blasts. They died by the dozens. Sam and his shield wall pushed forward, and the Conongan militia kept up a steady drumbeat of blaster fire on both sides.

We might just make it, Sam thought.

And then his luck ran dry.

CHAPTER 34

Fenra's assault had diminished the enemy fire to the point that Sam was finally afforded a clearer view of the battle-field, and what he saw was not what he had hoped to see. The forces on Sam's right flank had apparently lost all interest in the legionnaires coming at them from behind vibro shields. Instead they were now running to the building housing the chemical weapon.

So much for our distraction.

Sam was about to warn the captain over comms when things took an even worse turn. Fenra had just launched one of her last explosives when it was shot and detonated in midair—and not far in front of the shield wall. The already battered shields buckled under the concussive blast, and the legionnaires were tossed like rag dolls through the air.

Sam came to several yards back, not even knowing how he got there. One second, he was standing between Thompson and Doc, the next, he was hitting the ground and looking at sky. His head rang, and a pain in his chest told him a rib was bruised or broken. He could taste blood in his mouth. His armor was steaming from the heat of the blast.

Voices were shouting over the comm, or maybe just one voice. Sam couldn't tell. Nor could he make out any of the words. He looked around, his eyes feeling hazy... glassy. A wall of smoke filled the space between him and the rebel lines. Blaster fire emerged through the screen as the rebels fired blindly.

Sam rolled to the open doorway of a building to his right. He tried reactivating his shield, but it was good and truly gone. The war hammer was no longer on his back.

His world was a narrow-visioned nightmare of pain and incessant ringing, but that was slowly relenting, and soon he began to make out the voices over his comm.

"He's going for it, Troy. Let it go!"

It was Bean. Bean was the one shouting, and he wasn't the only one. So many voices filled the comm channel they were almost impossible to distinguish.

"Captain Zeno is down!" Moon shouted.

"Fall back to the palace!" Sola screamed.

Sam gritted his teeth and forced himself to his feet. He said a silent prayer and stepped out from the building. He sucked in a pain-filled breath to speak into the L-comm, but found he could do little more than let out a low moan.

He shook his head, and his vision cleared. He looked across the square, and saw his men.

Jarman was lying on the ground, unmoving. Doc was working on him. Thompson hugged dirt as blaster bolts scorched the air above him, and Fenra... she was a smoking pile of burned fur and body armor, but she was alive, struggling to her paws.

If it wasn't for the thick smoke covering the battlefield, blocking the enemies' view, they'd all be sitting ducks.

Sam took all of this in as the chatter over the comms intensified. He desperately wanted to take control of the situation... but found himself impotent. Barely capable of staggering and sipping in small breaths of air.

"Troy, don't do it!" Bean screamed.

"I can get it!" Troy roared back.

"Doc! Doc, we need you! The captain is down!" Moon shouted. "I repeat, Captain Zeno is injured!"

A fresh wind blowing in from the distant rice paddies sent some of the haze swirling away. Sam could now see Troy pinned down a block ahead from his own position. A dozen yards to his left, lying on the ground in clear view of both sides, was a dead rebel... holding the blue vial from the chemical weapon.

There was no sign of Bean, Moon, or the injured captain.

Sam could tell what Troy was thinking about doing, even without hearing Bean's warning cries over L-comm.

"Jarman is gone!" Thompson shouted into the comms. "The stupid son of a gun covered me after the explosion and took a round to the head. Why would he do that? Why would you *do* that, Jar? *I* should be dead! *Me!*"

Sam finally croaked out more than a groan. "Pull yourself together." Thompson would have to bury his feelings deep for the moment. "We have seconds before the wind clears enough smoke for the rebels to get accurate shots on us. Doc, help Thompson and get some cover."

He turned his attention to Troy. "Troy, report."

"We stormed the building, Sarge. One of the rebels took the canister and ran off, but I shot him in the back. I can get to it. I'm goin' for it!"

"Everyone that's still drawing breath, cover Troy!" Sam shouted. He scanned the area around him for anything he could use as a weapon. He found nothing but the worthless vibro shield on his arm. "Troy, I see you. I'm going to get to you as fast as I can!"

He bolted from his spot and pumped his legs. He spotted a discarded Anvil P9 halfway up the block. If he could reach that—and if it had a charge pack—at least he could provide some cover.

Time seemed to stand still. Every step was an eternity. Every breath an agony. The smoke was clearing, and the rebels were regrouping.

There were so many of them.

From an alley to the right, Bean appeared, his vibro shield activated. Moon and the captain were right behind him. Captain Zeno's helmet was missing, and he had one hand held to his neck, blood pouring between his fingers. Yet even through all that, he was on his feet.

Troy took off for the canister. Blaster rounds struck the ground all around him and sizzled off his shield. He scooped up the blue canister and started back toward the relative safety of the buildings, but his shield was taking a beating, and the glowing blue flickered, wavered. It was about to go.

"I don't believe this guy," Bean said over the comms. "Run faster, you idiot!"

Sam was watching all of this as he made his own run to the Anvil T9. He snatched it up and at once aimed it at the entrenched enemy no more than a block ahead of his position. "Let's go!" he yelled as he met a retreating Troy, Bean, Moon, and Captain Zeno.

"We've got you covered!" Thompson shouted. "Back! Back!"

The rebels were entirely focused in on the tiny legionnaire contingent now. They concentrated their fire. Zeno's shield was the first to fail under the withering onslaught. The wounded captain fell in behind the protection of the others.

Fenra appeared behind the Iron Wolves, half her fur missing and the skin underneath her white armor an angry red. The lyconlore's eyes spoke murder, and her teeth were bared as she charged not away, but *toward* the enemy lines.

"Fenra!" Sam shouted. "Get down!"

The lyconlore clearly had no intention of following that order. In her right paw she held the sack containing the large explosive—the big daddy meant for disabling the rebel's super cannon. She pulled her arm back and tossed it high into the air toward the world-eater.

Her aim appeared to be true, and she might just have the distance. They had a real chance of achieving both the objectives Captain Zeno had laid out for them, but they were much too close to the blast zone.

"Back!" Sam screamed, but there was no need. Every Iron Wolf was already sprinting as fast as they could. Fenra's heroics had been hard to miss.

Sam looked back over his shoulder as he ran, tracking the trajectory of the explosive. It fell behind the rebel lines, struck the ground with a roll, and came to rest near the super cannon.

It erupted like the hammer of the gods striking the very core of Cononga itself.

The ground shook, and the soil rolled under Sam's feet. It was all he could do to stay upright. The skies went dark with flames, smoke, and a geyser of dirt and debris.

So much smoke billowed over the rebel lines, it was impossible to tell if the charge had done its job. But whether the cannon was still operational or not, the rebels' fire had dropped to almost nothing. If Sam had a full contingent of Wolves, he would have led a charge right at this moment—and ended these rebels for good, but he had only a handful of men, some wounded, some unarmed. Retreat and regroup. It was their only option.

As the battered Iron Wolves neared the palace, Sola sent out Conongan soldiers to help them back inside. Sam waved away two medics who sought to inspect him right on the spot. "I can walk. I'll make it. Help the others."

Sam stood rooted to the spot, looking back toward the rebel lines. He couldn't tear his eyes away from the clearing smoke. He had to know if that cannon still stood.

It can't have survived. An explosion that size?

Seconds later the wind whipped up, and the grayish black smoke cleared enough to give Sam the verdict.

Like a statue promising destruction, the super cannon stood tall.

CHAPTER 35

"That's impossible," Bean cried over L-comm from the palace steps. "How can it still be standing?"

Sam was asking himself the same question. Had Fenra not gotten the bomb close enough to the target? In the end it didn't matter. The cannon stood, and if the *Breaker* was still in orbit, it would soon be lost—along with every hand on board.

Sam joined the rest of the group in the palace courtyard. The losses of Biel and Jarman ate away at him. Scores of Conongan militia had given their lives. Along with dozens of innocent civilians, including one bright-eyed boy.

How many more would need to die before this was all over?

Doc was busy attempting to stabilize Captain Zeno. "Easy. Easy, Captain."

Captain Zeno's neck and face were covered in a smear of crimson red. In spite of this, he was still trying to speak—probably to give orders.

Doc shook his head. "You can talk once I get this skin patch on there."

Troy handed Moon the vial of blue liquid like it was diseased. "I think you better be in charge of this, Moon."

Moon took it somberly. "I'll take care of it."

"Do you have a death wish or something?" Bean snapped at Troy as the leejes removed their helmets. "You could have died back there!"

"We all got to go sometime. I'm at peace with that." Troy shrugged and clapped his friend on the back. "Besides, you know me."

"Yeah, I do." Bean punched his friend in the shoulder. "That's why I worry."

"I got this, *muchacho*," Troy said with a grin. "We'll get back to see those babies of yours. Uncle Troy has to teach them some bad habits."

"It ain't over yet," Sam growled. "Quit yapping, get your buckets on, and be ready for a counterassault. It's what the Wolves would do if the tables were turned."

Looking down like scolded puppies, the two legionnaires again donned their helmets and looked to take up defensive positions.

It was dark now. The sun was gone, and the dark clouds were just beginning to empty their payloads of water on the planet below.

Sola came running up to Sam. "There's a lot of movement in their camp. I think the cannon is ready." She looked beyond weary, and her eyes held a deep sadness, but her voice remained strong. She hadn't broken. Not yet. "I think we'd better prepare for an assault."

"Already on it." Sam stepped up to Captain Zeno. "Sir? Plan B?"

Captain Zeno nodded.

That was all Sam needed.

"Troy!" he shouted. "Ready to test your piloting skills on that hunk of junk in the airfield?"

"I thought you'd never ask."

Sam turned back to the resident expert on getting around Cononga undetected. "Sola, you think you can sneak Troy out the back of the palace and get him some wheels?"

"I need to find Fenra."

"We've got her. She's all right. Getting patched up inside, but we're all gonna be in deep if Troy can't get out to the airfield right now."

"Yeah," Sola said. "Okay." She motioned for Troy to follow her.

"Get it in the air if you can," Sam said, thumping the private on his shoulder as he walked by. "We'll hold here. You did good today. You saved a lot of lives."

"Just doing my job," Troy said. "Or not doing my job, if you ask Major Roy, but not doing it *real well.*"

"Try not to crash," Bean said.

"If I do," Troy said, following Sola, "I'll make sure to land on your fat head. Can't miss it!"

Sam motioned to the rest of the legionnaires. "I want you all ready to KTF. Buttress the Conongans' lines. Make those rebels pay for every inch they push forward."

Lyn came out of the palace to join them. The liaison was covered in blood from his white apron to his gloved hands. The look on his face was one Sam recognized easily. He was in shock. Probably from what he had seen, what he'd had to do to save lives. The lives he hadn't been able to save. He nodded dumbly to Sam as he removed his gloves and sat down with a canteen of water.

Moon and Fenra joined the group a moment later. Everyone looked like ghosts of who they actually were. With sleep, hot food, and hotter showers they *might* look like people once again, but that was a long time coming, and at the moment, they seemed more likely to wind up in graves than showers.

"I didn't know it was like this," Lyn said to everyone and no one. "I didn't know. How could I have known?"

"No point now in playing what-ifs and maybes," Sam said, shaking his head. The pain in his chest was getting worse. Doc, or one of the medics, should probably take a look at him, but there was no time. One way or another, they were close to the end.

"I should have just reported the document was signed," Lyn said. He lowered his head, and tears splattered the inside of his glasses. "I should have... done something."

A moment of silence fell over the group.

Doc moved away from Captain Zeno and beckoned Sam over. "He's lost a lot of blood, and I'm not sure if his vocal cords are going to heal, but he'll live. He's one tough son of a gun."

"Doc says you'll make it, sir," Sam called over to the captain.

Captain Zeno nodded, his good eye taking in his sergeant. He pointed to his captain's insignia on his armor, then pointed to Sam.

"I got you, sir," Sam said. He understood. He would be the one leading from here on out.

A Conongan soldier came running into the courtyard, hopping over sandbags. His eyes were alive with fear. "They're coming! The rebels are attacking!"

Sam was beyond exhausted. Fatigue mixed with pain and remorse, but he didn't feel afraid. "Show me."

He ran with the Conongan soldier to the palace gates looking out over the square. The light rain had intensified to huge droplets of water that slid over and under his armor.

The enemy rebels were definitely stirring, but they were still gathering their ranks, not yet advancing from their positions.

How can there still be so many of them?

"We shootin' again?" Bean asked over L-comm. "What does this make, round four or five? I feel like a heavyweight boxer in a championship match. My body feels like it too."

"I hear that," Sam said. "We'll be all right. We'll make it."

"Yes, sir," replied Troy, sounding as though he didn't quite believe it.

Sam pushed away all doubt from his mind. "We hold the palace."

Sola appeared a moment later, out of breath. "Your private is on his way like a Tumerion out of hell. Now I need to check on Fenra."

"She's with Moon, but before you go—the rebels are preparing their advance. I want you to have your men open up on the rebels once they reach the halfway point across the square. Then fall back into the palace courtyard before you get overrun. Once you get inside, split your force equally to the east and west ends of the courtyard. I'll bring the Iron Wolves right up the middle with whatever vibro shields are still working."

Sola shook her head. "Those things aren't miracle weapons, you know. They barely handled the beating they took last time. I swear, they must feed you legionnaires crazy pills in the morning."

"And two before bed," Sam quipped.

"Fine," Sola said. "We'll get it done."

"Oorah?" Sam said.

"No."

"Oh, come on. You got to 'oorah' with us at least once. Even Fenra was letting out a few howls earlier."

"Yeah, well, Fenra also licks her private parts in public."

"Come on. Just once."

"Sorry. Not my thing."

"We're going to need it to be everyone's thing if we plan on living through this." Sam lifted his head to the darkening sky, inviting the crazy to guide him through what would come next. "*Oorah!*"

CHAPTER 36

The militia followed the plan perfectly. As soon as the rebels reached the middle of the square, the Conongans engaged them from entrenched positions. For now, they were keeping them back, but it wouldn't last. Once the rebels and sectoids brought up their full force, the outmanned militia would have to fall back.

"Sergeant," Troy said over L-comm, "I'm inside this old beaut. Gonna take me a while to figure out how to get her going, though. She is *ancient.*"

"Copy. Keep me up to date."

Sam had to believe Troy would find a way to get the bird in the sky and give them the advantage they needed, but he wasn't planning on that happening. He had to prepare for the worst.

With the skirmish picking up in the middle of the square, Sam took a moment to give the Iron Wolves one last pep talk. Just five legionnaires remained, including himself. Captain Zeno was out of the fight. Troy was on assignment. Biel and Jarman were gone.

That left Doc, Thompson, Hall, Bean, and himself.

That was it. That was what was left.

It would be enough. It *had* to be enough.

The rain alternated between torrents and light sprinkles, as if the weather couldn't make up its mind about what sort of misery it wished to dish out. Either way Sam's armor was drenched; only his synthprene undersuit kept his body dry.

"You all know me well," he said, using the comms but still shouting. His nerves prevented him from doing anything less. "You know my story. I've been busted from sergeant to corporal more times than I care to admit, and those of you who have been in the Wolves long enough know why."

He looked down. "I'm aware of my faults as a leader. I understand the danger I pose to this unit whenever I... lose control. If it weren't for Captain Zeno, I likely wouldn't even still be in the Legion. But the Iron Wolves... they have room for the head cases like me, and that's what I'm asking from all of you. We don't have the numbers or the equipment to fight this out the way we're accustomed. So I need something else from you instead. I need you Wolves to get lost in your ferocity.

"If it's our time to go, then it's our time to go. Nothing is going to change that. If today is that day, then we KTF until our graves come calling. We fight as long as our lungs draw breath—and then we get up and fight some more for the man standing beside us. Kill them first... kill them all!"

"Oorah! Oorah! Oorah!" the Iron Wolves howled back.

The Iron Wolves formed a center wedge at the palace gates, their vibro shields already beeping in warning that charge was low. The Conongan militia were falling back around them, the strategic withdrawal underway. Many of them looked scared.

Sam stood tall. These Conongan men would look to the Iron Wolves for leadership now more than ever. *Our courage is their courage.*

"The rebels made a mistake today!" Sam screamed on external comms. He wanted the militia to hear this too. "They think they're facing men! They're wrong—they're facing Wolves! Let's show them the difference!"

"Oorah! Oorah! Oorah!"

More Conongan soldiers ran past. Fenra and Sola were the very last to make it through a spray of enemy fire chasing at their heels.

Sam's heart felt like it was going to explode in his chest. Adrenaline caused his very muscles to shake. "Kill them all!" he roared.

"Oorah!"

The first wave of rebel soldiers crested the steps leading into the palace. It was clear they were under the impression they had already achieved a rout. They were not expecting to meet a wall of legionnaires blood-crazed and ready to annihilate. They were not expecting to be cut down by the Iron Wolves.

But more pressed through right behind them.

With a quick pull of his Anvil's trigger, Sam split open the head of a rebel soldier charging toward them, then pumped blaster bolt after blaster bolt through the armor of a sectoid mercenary until its chest looked like a collection of small craters. He dropped a third target before the Anvil clicked dry.

The Conongan militia on either side of the Iron Wolves boxed the enemy in with narrow alleys of concentrated fire, keeping the rebel militia from going around and flanking the shield wall. The dead rebels fell so quickly that their bodies were impeding the progress of those behind them.

Sam threw his empty Anvil to the ground and drew his blade, though he didn't look to have the opportunity to use it. *If they can't even get past their own dead, how are they going to get to us?*

A warning shout came from Doc Dobson. "Grenades!"

The rebels had realized they weren't going to take the palace courtyard with a blind charge of sheer force. Black steel balls of death came flying over the walls.

"Down!" was all Sam could scream before they detonated.

They sent the body parts of those already dead flying across the courtyard. Fortunately not a single grenade made it behind the Iron Wolves' shield wall, but two rolled to a stop just a few yards in front. They were enough to knock the legionnaires back in a mess of vibro shields and bloody rain.

"Get back on the line!" Sam ordered over the comms. "Get back—"

His right shoulder felt a pain so intense it took the breath out of him. The smell of his own burning flesh reached his nostrils as he went down.

Ahead of him, the men's vibro shields began to flicker and fade. They were about done. Doc grabbed him and dragged him behind the cover of a few sandbags.

"Let me check you out, Sarge."

Doc inspected the wound before cauterizing it with a flare. Skinpacks were all gone now. White-hot pain penetrated Sam's shoulder, causing him to howl with pain.

Captain Zeno's unnervingly hushed voice came over the comms doling out orders. It was good to hear he had his voice back. It was even better seeing the man himself race into the battle.

Sam leapt to his feet.

What he saw nearly broke his fighting spirit, if such a thing were possible for a legionnaire. The rebel grenades had disrupted the Iron Wolves' center wall, and a large push of insurgents and mercenaries had broken through the palace gate. Fighting was taking place in all corners of the courtyard now. Sectoids rode in on their huge insect-like mounts, bullying their way past sandbagged entrenchments. Injured beasts who'd lost their riders were adding to the chaos, attacking friend and foe indiscriminately.

From whatever defensive positions they could find, the Iron Wolves and Conongan militia poured fire at close range, but it seemed that for every rebel who fell, twice as many replaced him.

This is it, Sam thought as he ran to join his men. *This is when I die.*

The thought felt strange. Like death was some date he had marked on his calendar. Some appointment that was occurring right on schedule... and unexpected all the same.

He spotted Thompson, going down under a barrage of blaster fire.

He saw Captain Zeno, his neck bleeding through a partially dislodged skinpack, taking the head off a sectoid with the edge of his fading vibro shield. The captain pulled his sidearm and sent bolts into the eyes of the beast the sectoid had ridden on, but was then lost from view as the monster's body crashed down on him.

The other leejes were nowhere to be seen.

Oba, let me die well, Sam thought.

From the broken gates connecting the stairs to the palace courtyard, the green visage of Commander Tor appeared behind a four-man bodyguard. Each soldier carried a heavy blaster rifle.

Thank you, Oba.

"Tor!" Sam screamed like a maniac and raced straight toward the rebel commander he'd sworn to end on the field. He bottled his pain and used it as fuel. "Tor!"

Weapons fire sizzled around Sam's feet as he ran. A sectoid attempted to strike him with the butt of its rifle, but with a single swipe of his big leej knife, Sam separated the merc's arm from its body in a spray of green blood.

Sam didn't slow for a second. Being a moving target was the only thing keeping him alive right now. To stand still meant death.

He leapt over a low wall of alien corpses and barreled toward the alien commander, mere yards away now, his flickering blue shield leading the way.

The green-skinned aline saw Sam's charge. He met it with a cruel smile of recognition and pointed his weapon at the legionnaire. His guards did the same.

Leap of faith, Sam told himself.

He let the rage take him.

The battlefield seemed somehow distant. Distorted. Blurred. Shadowy.

Quiet.

Just the sound of the air circulating through his lungs.

His feet hitting the ground.

His blood pumping through his veins.

He hurled himself into the entourage. His armored shoulders and back crashed into two of the bodyguards like a wrecking ball. He whirled about them, savagely wielding his knife, slicing faces, spilling entrails.

Savage.

That's what it was. The Savage Wars revisited.

The Iron Wolves answering invasion with ferocity. Once again.

Sam used the last of his vibro shield's power to cut through armor, flesh, and bones as if they were nothing at all. The rebels screamed in terror.

Sam relished every moment.

So much blood covered Sam, he couldn't tell what was his own and what belonged to his enemies. His shield was dead, his gun was gone, but he still had his knife.

Tor stepped backward, fear in his eyes. The commander's last bodyguard was dead on the field.

Sam attacked.

The aline dodged and attempted to squeeze behind him. Sam pivoted, keeping Tor's weapon in close. He struck the rebel commander's wrist with a forceful elbow strike, and it clattered to the ground.

Now.

Now he had him.

He swung his blade up, slicing a gash in Tor's arm. He was about to bring his blade down for a final strike—when something cold, like a frozen needle, slipped through the side of his armor.

He looked down to see Commander Tor's free hand pressing the hilt of a knife between his ribs. The blade was buried deep in his torso.

Sam succumbed to a sudden, uncontrollable weakness. All the rage and strength fled his body in a wave of cold sweat. His legs gave out underneath him. He sank to his knees. His arms slumped. His knife slipped from his fingers and clattered harmlessly to the ground.

Sam could hardly breathe. Each lungful of air came at a cost that was becoming harder and harder to pay.

Commander Tor stood over Sam, sneering. "You stupid legionnaires should have run when you had the chance."

He leaned down, ripped the blade from Sam's side, and prepared to skewer him again. "Now you'll all die here on Cononga."

The air itself exploded above Sam. His first thought was that the cannon had destroyed *Breaker*, bringing an end to those Iron Wolves high above. Leejes who'd never even gotten the chance to look their attacker in the eye.

But then a more distinct noise descended over the battle. Weapons fire from a Republic drop shuttle.

The Wolves. They're here.

CHAPTER 37

An ancient, derelict craft stormed across the battlefield in a low buzz, obliterating the rebel forces with massive fifty-caliber slugs.

Sam couldn't believe his eyes, which were regaining sight as adrenaline—and new hope—surged through his body.

Neither could the rebel commander. Tor looked upward for a split second, his mouth sagging open, and this tiny window of opportunity was all Sam needed. With a quick roll he tripped the commander, sending them both rolling down the stone palace steps.

It was a long way to the bottom, but that was fine by Sam. He was the only one in armor. The longer the better.

Both aline and legionnaire fought for the hilt of the blade. The pouring rain, the disorienting tumble, the repeated jarring thuds against the stone, made it impossible for Sam to gain the upper hand.

But surely Tor was going to be worse for wear when they reached the bottom.

The sounds of the craft flying overhead and peppering the rebel forces played somewhere in the background, but they were distant in Sam's mind. His focus was on two thoughts only.

Get the blade. Slit Tor's throat.

The two opponents reached the bottom of the stairs and splashed into a pool of muddy water. But the fall had done its job. Tor's grip on the knife had loosened. Perhaps he'd hit his head a few times on the way down.

Sam grabbed the commander's knife hand and slammed it against the ground hard, knocking the weapon loose and sending it skittering away, lost beneath the surface of the water.

Then he pulled Tor close and rolled on top of him. The rebel screamed in rage and clawed at Sam's throat with both hands, but Sam weaved his arms inside Tor's, grabbed the rebel commander's head, and forced it hard to the left, so that his ugly face was submerged under the muddy water. With both palms on the side of Tor's face, he held it down.

Bubbles drifted to the surface—an underwater scream. Tor's hands, legs, his entire body spasmed, thrashing, fighting in vain to push Sam off. Sam's arms burned. The surge of strength he'd gained at the sound of the craft was fading, the blood still pumping out of the wound in his side, but there was no way he was going to let up now. The rage had him. He hung on.

Finally, Commander Tor's body went still.

The bubbles of air ceased.

Sam rolled off his enemy and flopped onto his back in the rainwater, feeling its coldness surge into his wound. He gazed up at the dark, rain-soaked sky, where a rust bucket of a craft flew back and forth over the battlefield, meting out destruction with twin cannons shooting old-school slugs.

It was the most beautiful thing he had ever seen.

He had completely tuned out the chatter on his comm, but now it found its way through to his consciousness. He heard...

... cheering.

The Conongan militia were cheering.

The battle had been won, but the cost...

He strained for word from any Wolves. He heard nothing. His eyes couldn't... couldn't focus on his HUD. Couldn't check for vitals.

Were they all dead?

Then let him join them.

Footsteps ran past him. Rebels, fleeing into the night. Leaderless and without air support. They ignored the legionnaire lying on his back at the bottom of the stairs. Perhaps they thought he was dead.

Perhaps he was.

"That super cannon is still powering up, Troy!"

Moon's voice. Over comms.

"You gotta take it out *now*!"

Sam turned his head to the right, almost lazily. The super cannon was in the distance, pointing skyward. It glowed a dull red.

"Hold on to your panties down there," Troy said, bringing the ancient starfighter around. "I got this."

Sam watched as the rust bucket strafed the ground leading toward the cannon, but its fire stopped before it reached the weapon itself.

"Uh, got a problem here," Troy said, the craft maneuvering in a tight U-turn. "Guns went dry."

Something was happening at the end of the world-eating super cannon. A red-hot ball was beginning to form, crackling with energy.

Whatever that weapon did… it was about to do it.

"Plan B," Troy said.

The starfighter turned.

Troy had set his ship on a collision course with the enemy weapon.

A tense silence descended over comms as the old relic picked up speed.

Then…

"This one's for the Wolves," Troy said. "You boys get on home, and if anyone asks… tell 'em I didn't forget nothin'."

Sam woke in a clean white room.

Am I dead?

A familiar, rancid odor filled his nostrils.

Fenra's heavy, gray head came into focus directly over him. Sola appeared next to the lyconlore a moment later.

"There he is." Sola nudged the grinning Fenra. "Go get the captain."

Fenra growled something, then disappeared from view.

"She says you look like death." Sola chuckled. "I'd have to agree with her."

Sam winced and looked around. He must be in the palace. Every inch of his body ached with a deep soreness.

Memories of the final battle—and Troy's sacrifice—flooded his mind.

"What... what happened?" He tried to get out of bed, and nearly fell. His head pounded and he fell back, as weak as he could ever remember. "Troy?" he asked.

Sola placed a hand on his shoulder. "Troy saved all of us. There's not a Conongan soldier, citizen, or Iron Wolf who doesn't owe him their life. Your men up on the *Breaker*, too."

"So the rebels..."

"Broken. Routed. I wouldn't have believed it could happen, but our intel is pretty clear. Whoever survived... they're not regrouping."

"How long have I been out?"

"Almost two days. You were bleeding out and had more injuries than a—a—well, you were ripped up pretty bad. We thought we lost you a few times. Fenra was heartbroken."

"Just Fenra, huh?" Sam asked with a twitch of his lips.

Sola's eyes twinkled. "Why? Who else would be missing you?"

Captain Zeno walked into the room.

Sola quickly stepped back. "I'll let you two do your legionnaire thing," she said. With a nod to the captain, she left the room.

"Sir," Sam said. He attempted to salute, but his arm hung limp and unresponsive. "I know we lost Thompson and Troy. The others?"

Captain Zeno spoke with a gravelly rasp. "All alive. Troy made sure of it." A metal brace had been fitted snugly against the side of his neck. Sam wondered if it was helping him talk.

"Alive and... well?"

Captain Zeno took a chair by Sam's bed. "Hall is recovering. Like you."

"Shouldn't we be in a brig right now?" Sam was trying to piece together the events that had transpired while he was out. "The Republic must have sent somebody. The *Breaker* at least, if not to help, then to force us to leave."

"It turns out Lyn's not the Senate liaison we thought he was. Or maybe he *was* exactly the person we thought... but after seeing war first-hand..." Captain Zeno shrugged. "It seems he told the Senate that he had confirmation that Cononga sat on a huge mine of larium ore. Of course, with that news, the Senate practically begged for President Gen to sign the papers."

"And... is that true?"

Lyn appeared at the door. "Could be. They have mines. Who knows what's in them? Glad to see you well, Sergeant."

"And you, Lyn." Sam turned back to Zeno. "Still, we disobeyed orders."

"Did we? Because the story I heard is that Cononga was already a part of the Republic when the attack happened. As such, it was the duty of the Iron Wolves to stand by our allies and defeat our mutual enemies."

"Huh," Sam said.

Lyn smiled. "The Iron Wolves are set to be stationed out by day's end. Delta Company from the Twenty-Second is due to replace you all."

"History is written by the victors," the captain said. "The Wolves will be remembered as heroes, which they are. Yourself included. And Troy will get the Order."

"Good," Sam said. "Not... not the being a hero part, but for Troy. His family and friends—the whole galaxy—should know what he did here."

"Oorah to that, Sergeant." Captain Zeno rose from his seat. "Rest up. There are more wars to fight. The Iron Wolves need you."

Sola reappeared in the doorway. Lyn cleared his throat. "Well, Captain, perhaps you and I should, uh..."

Zeno smiled. "Yes. Don't we have that..."

"Appointment," Lyn finished.

"Right."

Zeno and Lyn shuffled out the door, leaving Sam alone with Sola.

"Sounds like the Iron Wolves are leaving Cononga," Sam said, feeling suddenly melancholy at the prospect. He was going to miss Sola. Fenra, too.

Sola took a seat on the side of Sam's bed. "Didn't figure you'd stay."

Sam sighed. "Yeah. Life in the Legion, huh?"

"Yeah."

She leaned down and planted a long kiss on Sam's lips.

"What was that for?"

"For being crazy enough to save me. And my country." Sola looked at him thoughtfully. "The verdict is in."

"What verdict is that?" Sam asked, feeling a welcome flush from Sola's kiss.

"The Iron Wolves are still every bit the heroes they were in the Savage Wars."

Sam smiled. "Would you go so far as to say we're... legends?"

"I wouldn't go quite that far, but I would say..." She leaned down and whispered in his ear, her breath hot on his cheek, "Oorah, Sergeant Samson."

THE END

THE GALAXY IS A DUMPSTER FIRE...

HONOR ROLL

We would like to give our most sincere thanks and recognition to those who supported the creation of *Iron Wolves* by subscribing as a Galaxy's Edge Insider at GalacticOutlaws.com

Lee Abers
Guido Abreu
Elias Aguilar
Bill Allen
Tony Alvarez
Robert Anspach
Jonathan Auerbach
Sean Averill
Marvin Bailey
John Barber
Russell Barker
John Baudoin
Steven Beaulieu
Randall Beem
Matt Beers
John Bell
Daniel Bendele
Trevor Blasius
WJ Blood
Rodney Bonner
Ernest Brant
Geoff Brisco
Aaron Brooks
Brent Brown
Marion Buehring
Van Cammack
Shawn Cavitt

Kris (Joryl) Chambers
Cole Chapman
David Chor
Jonathan Clews
Alex Collins-Gauweiler
Michael Conn
James Connolly
James Conyer
Robert Cosler
Andrew Craig
Adam Craig
Phil Culpepper
Thomas Cutler
Alister Davidson
Peter Davies
Nathan Davis
Ivy Davis
Tod Delaricheliere
Christopher DiNote
Matthew Dippel
Ellis Dobbins
Andreas Doncic
Cami Dutton
Virgil Dwyer
William Ely
Stephane Escrig
Dalton Ferrari

Steve Forrester
Skyla Forster
Mark Franceschini
Richard Gallo
Christopher Gallo
Kyle Gannon
Michael Gardner
Nick Gerlach
John Giorgis
Justin Godfrey
Luis Gomez
Don Grantham
Gordon Green
Tim Green
Shawn Greene
Michael Greenhill
Jose Enrique Guzman
Erik Hansen
Greg Hanson
Adam Hartswick
Ronald Haulman
Joshua Hayes
Adam Hazen
Jason Henderson
Jason Henderson
Tyson Hopkins
Christopher Hopper
Curtis Horton
Ken Houseal
Jeff Howard
Mike Hull
Bradley Huntoon
Wendy Jacobson
Paul Jarman
James Jeffers
Tedman Jess

James Johnson
Randolph Johnson
John Josendale
Ron Karroll
Noah Kelly
Caleb Kenner
Daniel Kimm
Jesse Klein
Evan Kowalski
Byl Kravetz
Clay Lambert
Grant Lambert
Jeremy Lambert
Brian Lambert
Dave Lawrence
Paul Lizer
Richard Long
Oliver Longchamps
John M
Richard Maier
Brian Mansur
Deven Marincovich
Cory Marko
Pawel Martin
Lucas Martin
Trevor Martin
Tao Mason
Mark Maurice
Simon Mayeski
Quinn McCusker
Matthew McDaniel
Rachel McIntosh
Joshua McMaster
Christopher Menkhaus
Jim Mern
Pete Micale

Mike Mieszcak
Ted Milker
Alex Morstadt
Nicholas Mukanos
Andrew Niesent
Greg Nugent
Christina Nymeyer
James Owens
David Parker
Richard Parker
Eric Pastorek
Carl Patrick
Trevor Pattillo
Matthew Pommerening
Jeremiah Popp
Chancey Porter
Chris Pourteau
Joshua Purvis
Eric Ritenour
Walt Robillard
Daniel Robitaille
Joyce Roth
David Sanford
Landon Schaule
Shayne Schettler
Brian Schmidt
Andrew Schmidt
Alex Schwarz
Aaron Seaman
Phillip Seek
Christopher Shaw
Ryan Shaw
Brett Shilton
Vernetta Shipley
Glenn Shotton
Joshua Sipin

Daniel Smith
Tyler Smith
John Spears
Peter Spitzer
Dustin Sprick
Maggie Stewart-Grant
John Stockley
William Strickler
Kevin Summers
Ernest Sumner
Shayne Sweetland
Lloyd Swistara
Travis TadeWaldt
Daniel Tanner
Tim Taylor
Steven Thompson
Beverly Tierney
Matthew Titus
Jameson Trauger
Scott Tucker
Eric Turnbull
John Tuttle
Christopher Valin
Paden VanBuskirk
Paul Volcy
David Wall
Andrew Ward
Scot Washam
James Wells
Kiley Wetmore
Ben Wheeler
Scott Winters
Gary Woodard
Jason Wright
Brandt Zeeh
Nathan Zoss

DEAR READER

Amazon won't automatically tell you when the next Order of the Centurion Stand-alone (or Savage Wars, or Wraith Trilogy, or Galaxy's Edge Season 02) release, but there are several ways you can stay informed.

1. Enlist in our fan-run Facebook group, the Galaxy's Edge Fan Club, and say hello. It's a great place to hang out with other KTF-lovin' legionnaires who like to talk about sci-fi and are up for a good laugh.
2. Follow us directly on Amazon. This one is easy. Just go to the store page for this book on Amazon and click the "follow" button beneath our pictures. That will prompt Amazon to email you automatically whenever we release a new title.
3. Join the Galaxy's Edge Newsletter (inthelegion.com). You'll get emails directly from us—along with the short story "Tin Man," available only to newsletter subscribers.

Doing just one of these (although doing all three is your best bet!) will ensure you find out when the next Galaxy's Edge book releases. Please take a moment to do one of these so you can find yourself on patrol with the next group of brave legionnaires and experience with them their next gritty firefight!

Jonathan Yanez is the author of dozens of science fiction and fantasy novels. He's the winner of a Jack London Award for his contributions to literacy. Two of his series have been optioned for film. His latest work is currently under development being adapted into a mobile game. You can find out more about him by visiting www.jonathan-yanez.com

Jason Anspach is a best selling author living in Tacoma, Washington with his wife and their own legionnaire squad of seven (not a typo) children. In addition to science fiction, Jason is the author of the hit comedy-paranormal-historical-detective series, *'til Death*. Jason loves his family as well as hiking and camping throughout the beautiful Pacific Northwest. And Star Wars. He named as many of his kids after Obi Wan as possible, and knows that Han shot first.

Nick Cole is a dragon award winning author best known for *The Old Man and the Wasteland, CTRL ALT Revolt!,* and the Wyrd Saga. After serving in the United States Army, Nick moved to Hollywood to pursue a career in acting and writing. (Mostly) retired from the stage and screen, he resides with his wife, a professional opera singer, in Los Angeles, California.

Made in the USA
San Bernardino, CA
13 August 2019